THE PET *and* THE PENDULUM

The Misadventures of Edgar & Allan Poe

The Tell-Tale Start
Once Upon a Midnight Eerie
The Pet and the Pendulum

THE MISADVENTURES OF
Edgar & Allan Poe

BOOK THREE

THE PET *and*
THE PENDULUM

Gordon McAlpine

illustrations by Sam Zuppardi

VIKING
An Imprint of Penguin Group (USA)

VIKING
Published by the Penguin Group
Penguin Group (USA) LLC
375 Hudson Street
New York, New York 10014

USA * Canada * UK * Ireland * Australia
New Zealand * India * South Africa * China

penguin.com
A Penguin Random House Company

First published in the United States of America by Viking,
an imprint of Penguin Group (USA) LLC, 2015

LIBRARY OF CONGRESS CATALOGING-IN-PUBLICATION DATA
McAlpine, Gordon, author.
The pet and the pendulum / Gordon McAlpine ; illustrations by Sam Zuppardi.
pages cm.—(The misadventures of Edgar and Allan Poe ; book 3)
Summary: Back in Baltimore, twelve-year-old identical twins Edgar and Allan think they
have encountered the ghost of their great-great-great-great granduncle, Edgar Allan Poe,
asking them to solve his murder—but really it is their arch-nemesis, Professor Perry, looking
for revenge.
ISBN 978-0-670-78492-9 (hardcover)
1. Poe, Edgar Allan, 1809-1849—Juvenile fiction. 2. Twins—Juvenile fiction. 3. Brothers—
Juvenile fiction. 4. Revenge—Juvenile fiction. 5. Baltimore (Md.)—Juvenile fiction. [1. Poe,
Edgar Allan, 1809-1849—Fiction. 2. Twins—Fiction. 3. Brothers—Fiction. 4. Revenge—
Fiction. 5. Baltimore (Md.)—Fiction.] I. Zuppardi, Sam, illustrator. II. Title.
PZ7.M47825253Pe 2015
813.54—dc23
[Fic]
2014043909

Printed in the U.S.A.

10 9 8 7 6 5 4 3 2 1

Designed by Eileen Savage
Set in Stempel Schneidler Std

To my brother, Glenn—G. M.

To Tom and Lucy Horrell—S. Z.

A man who carries a cat by the tail

learns something he can learn in no other way.

—Adapted from Mark Twain

CONTENTS

SATELLITE MAY FALL OUT OF SKY

Scientists warn that satellite could reenter atmosphere and crash in populated region

HOUSTON, TX—NASA scientists announced today that the Bradbury Telecommunications Satellite, launched seven years ago, is exhibiting unusual changes in its orbit, which could bring the 1,390-pound object crashing back to Earth.

"The satellite has a fifty percent chance of reentering the atmosphere sometime in the next few days or weeks," said NASA communications director Maxmore Potkin. "Nonetheless, citizens should not panic, because most of the satellite will be incinerated upon reentry, making for little more than a spectacular light show."

Other scientists, however, suggest that if even a small portion of the satellite survives reentry and lands in a populated region, the impact could do tremendous damage. Where it might land is impossible to predict. Likewise, the cause for the change in its orbit remains a mystery. "Sometimes things happen that even rocket scientists can't explain," said Potkin.

The Bradbury Telecommunications Satellite first made news seven years ago, when its takeoff tragically claimed the lives of Mal and Irma Poe, NASA scientists who failed to leave the rocket during the countdown and were accidentally launched into space.

BACK TO SCHOOL

TWELVE-YEAR-OLD identical twins Edgar and Allan Poe—the great-great-great-great grandnephews of Edgar Allan Poe, famous nineteenth-century author of horror, suspense, and detective stories—sat in adjacent desks in their first period English class. Friends hovered around them, asking for details about the recent events in Kansas and New Orleans that had made the twins famous.

When the bell rang, their teacher, Mrs. Rosecrans, called the class to order, but no one paid her much attention. It was January 5, the first day back from winter break at Edwin "Buzz" Aldrin Middle School, so everyone was still in a holiday frame of mind.

Two weeks off will do that.

Of course, Edgar and Allan had been away from school much longer.

In mid-October, the Poe twins had been suspended from the entire Baltimore City School District on trumped-up charges. In the interim, they'd had amazing adventures. Nonetheless, they were glad to be back and happy to see their friends.

"Did no one hear the bell?" called Mrs. Rosecrans from the front of the room. Edgar and Allan noted that she'd lost weight since they'd last seen her—the glazed doughnut she habitually set on her podium had been replaced by an apple.

Good for her, the twins thought.

"Enough chattering!" she cried. Then she went on more gently: "Class, I understand you all want to welcome back Edgar and Allan. But we have a guest today."

At Mrs. Rosecrans's desk sat a dark-haired woman, well-dressed and possessed of a smile made prominent by a bright shade of red lipstick. She wore so much makeup that there was no way of guessing her age; she might have been anywhere between fifty and seventy. She waved a little sheepishly.

"Besides," the teacher continued as kids started back to their desks and the room finally settled, "I'm sure Edgar and Allan aren't the only ones to have had exciting adventures over vacation."

Stevie "The Hulk" Harrison, one of the twins' best friends, muttered sarcastically, "Sure, we've *all* experienced life-threatening criminal conspiracies, starred in a major motion picture, and discovered pirate treasure."

"Now, Stevie," answered Mrs. Rosecrans, tapping the metal podium, "let's not discount the excitement of ordinary life."

Stevie said nothing, having learned by being

repeatedly kicked out of class that it was better not to push her too far.

She cleared her throat. "Our guest this morning is Miss Re—"

But before she could get the whole name out, the dark-haired woman interrupted. "Please, Mrs. Rosecrans, nothing formal." She stood and nodded to the class. "Call me Birdy, kids. Everyone does."

It was clear that Mrs. Rosecrans didn't approve of adults using first names in a classroom, but she continued. "Class, this is Birdy from Roastmasters, a nationwide public speaking club." She turned to her guest and made a show of applauding, which coaxed a polite spattering of sleepy clapping from the class. "Birdy has generously offered to lend her expert analysis this morning to a few brief 'What I Did Over My Winter Break' impromptu speeches."

Public speaking in front of an expert—during first period?

The whole classroom sighed.

"So, who'll start?" Mrs. Rosecrans inquired.

No one raised a hand or even dared make a sound.

"Come, now. *Someone* must be willing to get us back into the spirit of learning." She looked around the room, finally pointing to Stevie "The Hulk." "You seemed full of vim and vinegar a moment ago, Mr. Harrison, so why don't you get us started?" She went to stand next to a bookcase.

"Great," Stevie mumbled as he squeezed out of his desk and went to the podium.

Edgar and Allan thought it too early in the day to inflict their mischievous will on the proceedings. So they sat back like two ordinary students.

They'd just listen.

At least until an opportunity for fun arose.

Birdy rolled her chair out from behind the cluttered desk to the side of the room opposite Mrs. Rosecrans. "Remember to speak slowly and clearly, and to hit every consonant," she advised. Then, with notepad in hand, she settled like a judge on a TV talent show.

Stevie stood behind the podium, looking from Mrs. Rosecrans at his right to Birdy at his left.

Surrounded.

"Enunciate," Mrs. Rosecrans said.

He turned to her and nodded.

"And stand up straight," added Birdy, removing a pencil from behind her ear.

Turning back toward the expert, he squared his shoulders.

"And relax!" the teacher insisted.

He turned once again toward Mrs. Rosecrans. "How am I supposed to relax like this?"

She acknowledged his difficulty. "All right, Mr. Harrison. Just tell us what you did on your winter break."

Stevie cleared his throat. "Um, over the holidays I went with my family to my aunt's house in Washington DC, where we ate lots of good food and watched some great games on TV."

"Details," Birdy interrupted, her hands fluttering like fledglings about her face. "It's details that engage your audience."

"OK," he murmured. "Turkey with cranberry-orange sauce and the Dallas Cowboys."

"Dramatic details!" Birdy's hands now flittered above her coiffed head. "Spice your story with conflict."

"Conflict?" he repeated. "OK. How about turkey with cranberry sauce *versus* the Dallas Cowboys?"

The class cracked up.

Birdy didn't skip a beat. "As your teacher said before, one can find excitement in any ordinary day's events."

Stevie sighed. "OK, um, one day my whole family went to the National Air and Space Museum, but the line was so long that my dad said we'd have to go back another time." He stopped and looked at Mrs. Rosecrans, who shook her head. "OK, I guess that's not very interesting or exciting," he acknowledged. Then his face brightened. In excitement, he rose up on his toes as he spoke. "Actually, the most interesting thing was that my family's cat, Roderick, was stolen by an evil professor and, along with my twin brother, I traveled all the way to Kansas to rescue him. How's *that* for exciting?"

At this, the class broke again into laughter, as Stevie had just described the now-famous incident that had set the Poe twins on their recent adventures.

"That's enough, Stevie!" Mrs. Rosecrans cried. "We want to hear about *your* time away, not Edgar and Allan's. The media has covered their exploits quite sufficiently. You may return to your seat." Then she turned back to the class. "Who'll go next?"

Again, no one raised a hand.

Mrs. Rosecrans pointed. "Katie," she announced.

Katie Justus was another of the twins' best friends. She was smart and stylish, her black hair braided with strings and beads. She moved gracefully to the podium. Then she took a short breath and, without a glance either right or left, started calmly. "Over my holiday, I went with my mom to a five-day ice carving class, where we began by carving simple ice pyramids with chisels and ended by carving ice swans, using little chain saws." Then a mischievous grin spread across her face. "And then, in Kansas, I not only rescued my cat, Roderick, at a broken-down *Wizard of Oz*–themed amusement park, but I also exposed the evil, catnapping professor as a wanted criminal and saw to his arrest."

"That's enough," interrupted Mrs. Rosecrans as the other students cheered. "Please, Katie. Not you, too."

Katie shrugged. "Well, it *is* an exciting story."

Mrs. Rosecrans stood and glared at Edgar and Allan. "The two of you are natural troublemakers."

The twins displayed their most innocent expressions.

"Don't think being famous gives you special privileges," she said.

"We don't," they answered truthfully, in unison.

"Besides, Mrs. Rosecrans," Edgar continued honestly, "you should know by now that when we put our minds to disrupting class, it's a lot worse than this."

"Well, that's true," she acknowledged. Frustrated, she turned and looked over the classroom. "Is there *no one* who wants to take this opportunity to learn from an actual public speaking expert?"

Riley McHuff raised her hand. She was every teacher's

dream student—so perfect and pliable that she could sometimes be a little aggravating to her classmates. "I'll be happy to engage in your public speaking exercise, Mrs. Rosecrans," she volunteered. "Particularly as we have such a distinguished guest here to comment."

Mrs. Rosecrans looked relieved. "Thank you, dear."

Riley took her place at the podium.

"'My Winter Break, by Riley McHuff,'" she started, formally introducing her impromptu speech.

"Excellent poise and introduction," Birdy commented.

After a pause, Riley grinned uncharacteristically. "So, after solving the crime in Kansas, I made a movie in New Orleans, where I discovered the lost pirate treasure of the Lafitte brothers and managed to solve a two-hundred-year-old murder, to say nothing of also capturing two criminals who turned out to be the mother and daughter of the evil professor, who, in the meantime, had escaped from jail and disappeared somewhere in Asia—"

The class erupted in laughter and cheering.

"Enough!" Mrs. Rosecrans cried, defeated.

Birdy shook her head with a smile.

Riley received many pats on the back as she returned to her seat.

Mrs. Rosecrans turned back to Edgar and Allan. "I

give up. It seems all anyone wants to talk about is you two."

The twins shrugged identically.

"So, which of you would like to come up to tell the class something they don't already know from the news?"

The Poe twins looked at each other.

Allan or Edgar?

Actually, it didn't matter, as neither was more nor less inclined than the other toward public speaking. And this was not the only area in which they shared identical views—actually, the Poe twins felt the same about *everything*. This was not because they lacked opinions. Rather, their identical responses resulted from a secret that almost no one realized—not their best friends nor even their aunt Judith and uncle Jack, who'd raised the twins since their scientist parents had been killed in a NASA accident seven years before.

This was their secret: Edgar and Allan were identical on the inside as well as the outside.

The boys' two minds acted as one. This made determining which boy was which impossible, even for the Poe twins themselves. Whatever one knew, the other also knew instantaneously, however far apart they were.

With two brilliant minds working as one, they could acquire and analyze a far greater amount of information than any single mind.

Even their famous great-great-great-great granduncle had never conceived of such an oddity. And he had written about many odd things.

Still, Edgar and Allan had never been able to figure out why they were this way.

Only their nemesis, the disgraced fugitive Professor S. Pangborn Perry, was truly aware of their secret, and he was bent on using it for his own nefarious purposes. But in Kansas he had been foiled by the twins' quick thinking.

"Well, boys?" Mrs. Rosecrans pressed.

"I'll go," Allan said, rising from his desk and starting up toward the podium.

ᏽᏽ💀ᏽᏽ

WHAT THE POE TWINS DID NOT KNOW...
ENCRYPTED PHONE TEXT FROM PROFESSOR S. PANGBORN
PERRY TO UNDERGROUND QUANTUM INDUSTRIES, INC.
(RUSH ORDER DEPARTMENT)

> The machine I am contracting you to build will con-
> sist of a room-size device able to accommodate two
> twelve-year-old boys tied face up, side by side, on a
> flat surface. A large blade will be suspended above
> the boys from the top of the device, like a pendulum.
> This blade must be sharp enough to cut one or the
> other of the boys in half (to be determined randomly,
> with precise fifty-fifty odds). The other boy must sur-
> vive unharmed. I will fax you the blueprints so that you
> can begin soon. I will need delivery within the week.

THE TRUTH ABOUT GHOSTS

THE classroom hushed as Allan took his place at the podium.

"My only correction to the outstanding speeches we just heard," Allan began, "is that in both Kansas and New Orleans, our cat, Roderick Usher, rescued my brother and me just as surely as we rescued him."

"Good clarification, Allan," Mrs. Rosecrans commented. "But tell us something new, please."

First, he considered talking about Em and Milly, whom he and Edgar had met in New Orleans while shooting *A Tale of Poe*. Like Edgar and Allan, the girls were twelve-year-old twins with a famous nineteenth-century literary ancestor: the poet Emily Dickinson. They had been critically important in the discovery of the buried pirate treasure and the settling of a centuries-old score with the pirate Pierre Lafitte. But Em and Milly already had been on the news.

And then Allan hit on a better idea.

"I want you all to imagine a dark cemetery," he said.

His classmates leaned forward.

Birdy set her pencil down and listened.

"Picture above-ground crypts, decayed and weathered houses of the dead," he continued. "Of course, you've already heard that we discovered the pirate treasure in one such crypt. And you want to hear something more. So I'll share a few details we *didn't* tell the media. . . ."

He paused for effect.

"Ghosts are real," he whispered, just loud enough for all to hear. The quiet made it all the more dramatic.

And then there was a loud *bang!*

The entire class jumped out of their chairs, and almost out of their skins.

At his desk in the back of the room, Edgar smiled and shrugged. "Oops," he said, picking up the heavy textbook he had "accidentally" dropped on the linoleum. "Clumsy me."

There was a collective sigh of relief.

Allan settled himself once more at the podium. "Well, as I was saying, my brother and I discovered some important new facts about ghosts during our hours in the Saint Louis Cemetery in New Orleans." He paused and gazed at the students. "You might be interested."

They nodded in assent, their eyes wide.

Even Mrs. Rosecrans looked interested.

Birdy was agog, no longer an expert, but a member of the audience.

"Not everyone who dies becomes a ghost," Allan explained calmly. He was the expert now. "Most of the deceased move on to some mysterious place that, unfortunately, my brother and I know nothing about. You see, our sources, who were two-hundred-year-old ghosts . . ." He paused momentarily, noting how the whole room seemed to be holding its breath. "Well, since these ghosts had never moved on, they could not describe what lay beyond."

"Why didn't they move on?" asked Stevie.

Mrs. Rosecrans was sufficiently interested to not scold him for speaking out of turn.

"The spirits of those who are murdered and whose killers go unrecognized are trapped near wherever the crime occurred," Allan answered. "It is injustice that keeps them here as ghosts."

"For how long?" asked Katie Justus.

Allan shrugged. "Until someone either publicly iden-
tifies their murderer or avenges the crime."

"So, your two-hundred-year-old sources had been . . .
murdered?" Stevie ventured.

"Yes, but my brother and I, along with our friends Em
and Milly Dickinson, set matters straight by identifying
their murderer."

"Pierre Lafitte," muttered Mrs. Rosecrans, as caught
up in the story as everyone else.

"Exactly," Allan said.

"And now they've moved on to the next place?" asked
David Litke, who was usually more interested in pirates
than ghosts.

Allan nodded.

"And what do ghosts look like?" Birdy asked.

"They look just like you and me. Except they can do
things like remove their heads and hold them in their arms.
But our particular ghost friends, Clarence and Genevieve
Du Valier, didn't really *like* to make spectacles of themselves. Spooking the living held little interest for them."

"Remove their heads?" Mrs. Rosecrans interrupted
doubtfully.

"Why not? They're ghosts," replied Allan.

"So if they don't spend their time spooking humans, what do they do?" Katie asked.

Edgar spoke up from the back of the room. "Mainly, they wait."

"For what?" asked Riley McHuff.

"Justice," Edgar said.

The room was silent.

Mrs. Rosecrans turned to Allan. "Thank you for your talk," she said. "Quite an imaginative fantasy. It must run in the family, considering your famous ancestor. You may return to your seat now, Allan."

Fantasy?

Allan only shook his head. Some people were impossible to persuade, being so distracted by mere facts that they were unable to perceive the truth behind the facts. That was Mrs. Rosecrans.

It didn't make her a bad person.

Just an ordinary adult.

"I'm all finished here," Birdy announced, nervously putting her notepad and pencil into her handbag and starting rapidly for the door.

"Must you go already?" Mrs. Rosecrans inquired with surprise.

But Birdy, pale and anxious to leave, did not answer her.

At least some adults believe, the Poe twins thought.

But why did they always believe there was something to fear from the dead?

Edgar and Allan knew better. They had never met a gentler couple than Monsieur and Madame Du Valier of old New Orleans, even when the pair was headless. No, the dead were all right.

Judging from the Poe twins' recent experiences, it was the living who could be dangerous.

After the bell, as the other students started off to their second period classes, Mrs. Rosecrans approached Allan and Edgar.

"We didn't mean to scare Birdy out of the room," Allan said before she could reprimand them.

The teacher waved away his concern. "That's not what I want to talk to you boys about," she said, leaning on a nearby desk.

The twins had never seen her adopt such a casual posture.

"It seems Birdy's a bit of a *chicken*," she continued, chuckling.

The twins looked at each other. They'd never heard her crack a joke either.

What was up?

She collected herself. "I wanted to ask you two if you're all right," she said.

"Oh, Professor Perry's still in hiding somewhere in Asia," Allan answered confidently. "He wouldn't dare show his face in this country. So don't worry, Mrs. Rosecrans."

She shook her head. "Actually, I was wondering how you two are holding up with this recent news about your parents' satellite."

"Oh," the boys said.

Many times these past seven years, Edgar and Allan had looked into the night skies—most recently from a dark Kansas cornfield—to locate among the stationary stars the tiny, orbiting speck of light that was their mom and dad's tomb. It was only periodically visible, usually soaring over other longitudes or latitudes, but with simple calculation its appearances were as predictable as the tides. The twins never lost an opportunity to observe it, though their feelings were always complex.

Naturally, they loved and missed their parents. So

it was always sad. But there was also a comfort in the predictability of the orbit, a sense of permanence that surpassed the carved names and dates on headstones, which, after all, eventually are worn away to blank slates.

"Why do you ask?" Edgar inquired.

"Well, all your talk just now about ghosts," Mrs. Rosecrans started. "It made me wonder if, psychologically, you weren't really talking about . . . well, if you weren't kind of reaching out."

"But everything Allan said was true."

Mrs. Rosecrans shrugged. "That may be. Still, I'm asking because I care about the two of you."

"You do?" they asked.

She'd once given them detention three times in one day.

"Of course," she said softly. They could see from her eyes that she was telling the truth.

In a way, this was even more surprising than meeting real ghosts.

"Thank you, Mrs. Rosecrans," said Edgar.

Allan nodded. "Of course, we'd prefer that the satellite not return to Earth like some kind of erratic bomb. But . . . what can we do?"

"I understand," she replied.

"But we're OK," he added.

A few weeks before, they might not have taken it so well. But it was a consolation to have met Clarence and Genevieve Du Valier. The kind couple was still happy to be together, even if they'd been trapped for two centuries in the general vicinity of their moldering grave. Edgar and Allan believed that their own parents were still together too . . . somewhere. And unlike the Du Valiers, the boys' mother and father had been victims of an accident. They would have moved straight to whatever lay beyond, without any need for justice to be meted out.

"The satellite may contain our parents' flesh and bones—" Edgar started.

"—but not their spirits," concluded Allan.

"That's a good way to see it, boys," Mrs. Rosecrans said.

"Besides, we don't need the occasional, orbiting appearance to be reminded of Mom and Dad," Edgar said.

"We never forget them in the first place," Allan added.

Mrs. Rosecrans blinked, as if she had something in her eyes.

"Are *you* all right?" Edgar asked her.

Students for her next class started coming into the room. Mrs. Rosecrans stood up straight and quickly collected herself.

"Now, you two get to class," she told the twins, her tone once again authoritarian. "There'll be no late pass for either of you, so you'd better move it!"

"Yes, ma'am," they said.

Glancing back as they left, the twins noticed that their teacher had taken her position at the podium and had seemed to return to normal.

But now Edgar and Allan knew the truth about her.

She was far better than normal.

WHAT THE POE TWINS DID NOT KNOW ...
ENCRYPTED E-MAIL MESSAGE STRING

From: newpoe@The-poes.net

Sent: Mon, Jan. 5, 9:53 am

To: Birdyreynolds@The-poes.net

Subject: RE: INTELLIGENCE

Birdy,

Your information is quite useful.

Professor P.

- -

> **From:** Birdyreynolds@The-poes.net

> **Sent:** Mon, Jan. 5, 9:51 am

> **To:** newpoe@The-poes.net

> **Subject:** RE: INTELLIGENCE

> Dear Professor,

> You'll be delighted to learn that my visit bore

> fruit. It seems the twins believe that any victim

> of an unsolved murder is doomed by "injustice"
> to haunt the vicinity of his or her death until the
> murder is either avenged or publicly solved. The
> twins are *quite* convincing in this ghost business
> (I must admit to having felt a momentary chill).
> But regardless of the accuracy of their belief, I
> thought you might be able to use this intelligence
> to manipulate them in some way, seeing as your
> cleverness knows no bounds.

> Sincerely,

> "Birdy" (your faithful new eyes and ears)

> P.S. The teacher suspects nothing of my actions
> or true intentions.

HOME SWEET HOME

IT had been three weeks since the Poes had returned from New Orleans to Baltimore and their nineteenth-century white clapboard house. Outwitting criminals on the road trip—three generations of the nefarious Perry family and a long-dead pirate—had been exhilarating for Edgar and Allan. Finding treasure and making a movie had been fun too. Aside from being kidnapped, Roderick had seemed to enjoy it all. And Uncle Jack and Aunt Judith now had many good stories to share with friends in their bowling league. Still, the twins were relieved to be back home with their projects and experiments.

This weekend, they planned to finish the cat door that would allow Roderick to move freely between the house and the screened porch.

It would be no ordinary, pet store–bought door.

Instead, the boys built an eighteen-inch-high scale replica of the ancient doors of Notre Dame Cathedral in Paris. There were cat-height motion detectors on either side, so the portal slid open automatically at Roderick's

approach. A snippet of Beethoven's Ninth Symphony played whenever he passed through.

"Roderick's a cat," Uncle Jack commented when he saw it in action. "Not the king of France!"

"Now, Jack, you have to admire the boys' ingenuity," Aunt Judith responded, setting down her Saturday morning grocery shopping and kneeling to touch the intricately carved antique French oak doors.

"Well, maybe if their efforts were going into homework or something . . ." Ordinarily, their uncle was more supportive of his nephews' independent activities. But today he was grumpy—with winter break over, he had no further excuse for not taking down the Christmas lights, as Aunt Judith had been asking him to do since New Year's Day.

"Homework?" Allan responded in disbelief. "We finish our homework every day on the bus ride home, Uncle Jack."

"But that's just fifteen minutes."

"Which leaves us plenty of time to chat with the bus driver, who used to be a navy deep-sea diver," Edgar said.

Uncle Jack shook his head. Sometimes he couldn't keep up with the twists and turns of conversations with his nephews. But neither could he argue with their excellent grades.

"Roderick may not be the king of France," Aunt Judith observed as the cat paraded out to musical accompaniment, and then back in, "but with that kind of entrance, he might be king of cats."

"The doors' craftsmanship *is* undeniable," Uncle Jack acknowledged. He bent and petted Roderick, who purred in appreciation. "It's a darn good doorway for an ordinary cat."

Roderick stopped purring. He sat and puffed out his chest, which bore a distinctive figure eight of white fur.

Allan's and Edgar's jaws dropped. "Ordinary?" they objected simultaneously.

"Well, um . . ." Uncle Jack stammered, realizing that his grumpy mood might have trapped him in a corner. "What I meant was that Roderick is only 'ordinary' because *all* cats are extraordinary."

The twins looked at him doubtfully.

"If that's so, then the word 'extraordinary' has no meaning," Allan observed.

"Remember, dear," Aunt Judith reminded her husband, patting his shoulder reassuringly, "Roderick does know how to play dead. And he is an expert at untying knots. That's pretty extraordinary."

"And that's not the half of it," Edgar and Allan said in unison.

Roderick *was* possessed of unusual skills. His ability to play dead and to untie knots had twice saved Edgar's and Allan's lives. His latest trick, learned in the back-seat of the Volvo wagon on the way home from New Orleans, was to tap his front paws in time with music on the radio. His favorite number was the old surf instrumental "Wipe Out," with its distinctive drum solo.

"OK," Uncle Jack admitted, "he *is* extraordinary."

Roderick purred once more and paraded regally out the tiny cathedral doors.

"Well," Allan said in a conciliatory manner as the music played, "it *is* true that all cats are extraordinary *in their own ways.*"

"Exactly," said a clearly relieved Uncle Jack. "That's what I meant."

"Yes, that's what we thought you meant," Edgar said, high-fiving their uncle.

The twins admired the new cat door for a moment. Then they turned to each other.

"Next?" they said.

The rest of the day was spent constructing a telescope with the same materials and design Galileo had employed in the early 1600s. Made of wood and leather with a convex main lens and a concave eyepiece (which the twins had ground using Aunt Judith's kitchen utensils), the instrument was exactly 980 millimeters long, or roughly three feet. When they took it up on the roof, they did not expect to see farther than they'd see with even an ordinary pair of binoculars. The old design was outdated in that regard. Rather, their experiment was to determine if, by using ancient techniques, they might be able to see back through time.

It was a long shot, they knew.

But then, the remarkable coordination that made Edgar and Allan two boys with one mind . . . that was a long shot too. So who was to say what was impossible?

Unfortunately, the telescope didn't see backward through time—except in the way of all telescopes, which capture light that has taken time to travel from a distant image. Still, the experiment was not a failure. It had simply disproven one of many theories that now would not have to be tested again, which was one way science moved forward—by just moving on.

As did the Poe twins.

On Sunday, they completed their half-finished work on three-dimensional backgammon and their preliminary design for shoes that used kinetic energy to melt snow from driveways, eliminating the need for shovels and plows (the shoes' wearer, however, would have to be either a master of tap dance or an Olympic-caliber athlete).

They'd caught up with all their leftover projects.

This enabled them now to give their full attention on Sunday night to their new and most important project—finding a way to direct the path of their parents' gradually descending satellite so that it would land in an ocean or uninhabited desert, thereby harming no one on the ground. Their parents had lost their lives because of the satellite, and those two lives were already two too many.

As soon as the NASA scientists realized the impending disaster, they had sent a letter to the Poe family, explaining the difficulty:

Ironically, what makes the satellite's reentry and landing impossible to control from Earth is that the nine-digit security code necessary to access the craft's stabilizers was known only to the designers, Mal and Irma Poe, who, of course, are tragically no longer with us. Further complicating matters is that entering any inaccurate series of numbers *even once* permanently disables the remote system. This is why we cannot use computers to send the one billion numerical possibilities to the satellite to unlock its navigational capacity. . . .

But the boys weren't easily discouraged.

They stayed up late Sunday night trying to figure out what nine-digit number their parents might have chosen as the code.

Likely, they'd have picked a number easy to remember.

Therefore, it could be a combination of Mal's and Irma's birthdays (3-14-71 and 5-2-69) or their respective addresses as children, or their address and ZIP code at the time of their deaths, or some combination of their years of high school and/or college graduations, or it could be their beloved twins' birthday and identical birth weights, or the twins' classroom numbers in kindergarten through second grade, or . . .

The possibilities were, unfortunately, endless.

And, setting numbers aside, their parents might have chosen one or more words consisting of nine letters that corresponded to the digits on a telephone. For example:

PoeFamily = 763326459

RTwinBoys = 789462697

ReadEAPoe = 732332763

Or something altogether unpredictable, like:

Anteaters = 268328377

So, even if we were *allowed multiple guesses, we might never guess right*, the boys conceded.

Edgar and Allan weren't accustomed to being stumped.

Hours later, after finally falling asleep, the twins dreamed of sitting on kitchen chairs before bowls the size of oil drums filled with alphabet soup. They each spooned in slurp after slurp of the broth and the little pasta pieces shaped like numbers and letters. Innumerable slurps. But even all this slurping failed to satisfy what became an increasingly ravenous hunger. And the bowls never seemed to empty. Edgar and Allan were relieved of this nightmare only when their alarm clock went off.

Rarely had they been so glad for the arrival of Monday morning.

When the twins got home from school that afternoon, Aunt Judith looked up from where she sat at the kitchen table and asked, "So, how was your day?" She was working on a needlepoint version of Rembrandt's *Night Watch* while listening to an audiobook about the lives of women in Renaissance times.

"Fine," they answered, as they usually answered.

"A little more information, *please*," Aunt Judith insisted, as she usually insisted.

Roderick sauntered into the kitchen, as cool as ever, only his smiling eyes giving away his enthusiasm for the return of his two favorite human beings.

The boys petted him as he brushed against their ankles.

After a moment, Allan made for the pantry.

Edgar made for the fruit bowl.

Aunt Judith set her needlepoint down and shut off the audiobook. "Well?"

"They've moved the human skeleton in the biology lab into a locked glass case," Allan said, smiling.

Months before, the twins had surreptitiously re-arranged the bones into a creature so monstrous that the biology teacher, Mr. Parker, had suffered an anxiety attack when he and the class entered the room.

"As if a little lock on a glass case could keep us from . . ." Edgar began. He stopped.

"From what?" Aunt Judith's eyes narrowed.

"Nothing," they answered.

Their aunt was clearly unconvinced.

"How was *your* day?" Allan asked, turning to her with a jar of peanut butter in his hand.

Edgar arranged neatly sliced apples on a plate.

"I got a phone call from the Dickinsons," she said.

The Dickinson family had been in Mexico and Central America since the movie finished shooting in New Orleans. They traveled the world whenever Dr. and Dr. Dickinson, who were college professors at Johns Hopkins University in Baltimore, had time off.

"How are they all doing?" Allan asked as he spread peanut butter on the apple slices.

"They've had a good trip. They're coming home soon."

"Great," the boys said.

Em and Milly had been sending them postcards: Mayan pyramids in the jungles of Mexico and Guatemala; colorful markets and colonial churches in El Salvador; sad-eyed sloths in the rain forests of Costa Rica; white, sandy beaches in Nicaragua . . . Milly, the techie of the two, would have preferred e-mail, instant messages, or texts, but Edgar and Allan were still forbidden to use any

electronic devices, having accidentally knocked out the electrical grid for the entire city of Baltimore last year while hacking the Internet.

"And that's not all," Aunt Judith continued.

The boys joined her at the table, setting the plate of peanut-buttered apple slices at the center.

"Thank you, boys," she said. But before taking one, she removed a sealed nine-by-twelve-inch manila envelope from the needlework bag at her feet. She set the envelope on the table.

"I found this an hour ago with the rest of the mail," she explained. "However, as you can see, there's no postage, so it must have been hand-delivered."

The boys were impressed with her observational skills.

"And it's addressed to you two," she continued. "No return address."

These days, their ordinary fan mail was delivered to the movie studio's publicity department, sparing the twins hours of autograph requests.

This was something different.

"Well, open it," Aunt Judith said.

Edgar tore the envelope across the top and slid a well-worn hardcover book onto the table.

"Who's it from?" she asked, selecting a peanut-buttered apple slice.

Allan picked up the book, riffling the pages to see if a note might fall out.

Nothing.

Edgar looked inside the envelope. No note.

The boys shrugged.

"Have you two read this one?" she asked.

"Naturally," they answered. They'd read almost everything written about their great-great-great-great granduncle.

"As I recall, this biography is from the early nineteen

twenties," Allan said, flipping to the copyright page. "Yes. Nineteen twenty-three."

"So why would someone send it to you anonymously?" Aunt Judith asked before taking a bite of apple.

Edgar and Allan had a long history of receiving mysterious messages from . . . someplace. Until recently, they'd gotten identical fortune cookies whenever the family dined at Chinese restaurants. Even more uncannily, the fortunes had carried accurate messages (except for instances of typographical errors, in which case the fortunes had proved exactly the *opposite* of the truth).

The boys had also discovered cryptic personal messages in tourist brochures, newspaper headlines, a misprinted section of the script for the movie in New Orleans, and personalized license plates in three states. Many of these messages were warnings. That Edgar and Allan didn't know where they came from didn't mean the twins took them any less seriously.

And now, here was an old biography of their famous forebear.

"Maybe somebody's just passing along an old book they figured you two would like," Aunt Judith suggested, wiping her fingers.

"Maybe," the boys said doubtfully.

Edgar riffled through the book. There were no markings, no clues. It looked like they'd have to reread the whole thing, looking for a subtle message in the text.

Or perhaps not.

"There it is!" Allan shouted.

"What?" Aunt Judith asked.

"A page is missing," Edgar explained.

"Torn out?"

Allan shook his head. "Sliced cleanly, as if by a razor blade."

"So, what does that mean?"

"The excised leaf is pages 277 and 278," Edgar muttered.

"So?" she asked.

For a moment the boys were silent.

Could it have something to do with the mysterious nine-digit code?

"Added together, 277 and 278 equal 555," Edgar observed. "Do you think 277278555 could be the code?"

"Could be," Allan acknowledged. "Of course, we can't afford to be wrong."

Edgar agreed. "Multiplied, they equal 77,006. Being only five digits, that doesn't get us anywhere."

"You two do have a way with numbers," Aunt Judith observed.

With two coordinated brains acting as one? Child's play.

"Dividing one by the other you get .996402877 or 1.00361010," Edgar said.

Aunt Judith's jaw dropped. "You did *that* in your head?"

"Just out to nine digits," Edgar said.

"Because that's all we need," Allan added. Then he turned to his brother. "But which set of nine?"

Edgar sighed helplessly.

"So what do all those numbers mean?" Aunt Judith asked.

"Maybe nothing," Edgar answered.

"A message may be written in ordinary words on that missing page," Allan elaborated. "A message that refers to some other mystery altogether."

"What do you mean, some *other* mystery?" Aunt Judith asked worriedly. "And why would someone who wanted you to see a message cut it out of the book?"

"To draw our attention to it," Allan said.

She shook her head. "In that case, why not just leave the page *in* and underline the important part?"

The boys looked at each other. *Why not?*

"There must be more to it than meets the eye," Allan proposed.

"Like what?"

"Adventure," Edgar said.

"Oh no, not more of that . . . please." Danger didn't agree with Aunt Judith, though she was slightly better suited to it than Uncle Jack. "Haven't we had enough?"

"We need to find that page," Edgar said.

"But since we don't own a copy of this book . . ."

Edgar turned to his aunt. "We have to go to the library. Main branch. Right now."

"To pursue this . . . mystery?"

The twins got up from the table. "Of course not, Aunt Judith," said Edgar.

"We have to go there to do our homework," Allan said. "School's back in session, after all."

"But I thought you said you always did your homework on the bus," she said suspiciously.

The twins shook their heads. "Special project."

And with that, they were out the door.

WHAT THE POE TWINS DID NOT KNOW...
FAX FROM PROFESSOR S. PANGBORN PERRY TO
UNDERGROUND QUANTUM INDUSTRIES, INC.
(RUSH ORDER DEPARTMENT)

Below, you will find the aforementioned blueprint.

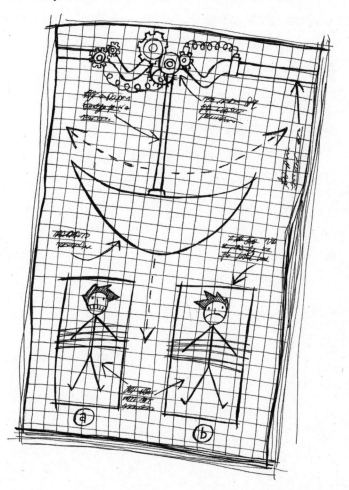

For additional clarification, you may refer to the Edgar Allan Poe story "The Pit and the Pendulum," from which I have taken these helpful, descriptive quotes:

. . . a huge pendulum such as we see on antique clocks . . .

. . . its nether extremity was formed of a crescent of glittering steel, about a foot in length from horn to horn; the horns upward, and the under edge evidently as keen as that of a razor . . . and the whole hissed as it swung through the air . . .

I saw that the crescent was designed to cross the region of the heart . . .

Mr. Poe in the Great Beyond

Edgar Allan Poe had been dead now for 165 years, and had recently suffered a discouraging string of demotions in the Celestial Office Building. His boss, Mr. William Shakespeare, did not make life—or, rather, death—easy for him.

First, Mr. Poe had been transferred out of the Fortune Cookie Division, where for years he'd communicated advice, occasionally misprinted with near-disastrous effects, to his beloved great-great-great-great grandnephews, Edgar and Allan, down on Earth. His next demotion, to the License Plate Division, offered him only the opportunity to send the twins general warnings about the evil plots swirling around them (for example, "DNGR4U2").

And this latest demotion was even more challenging: the Animal Languages Division.

Here the surrounding cubicles were occupied not by other writers—like Mr. Walt Whitman (Gardening Supplies Catalog Division), Mr. Mark Twain (Street Signs Division), or Miss Emily Dickinson (Greeting Cards Division). Instead, the cubicles were occupied by cows mooing, lions roaring, horses whinnying, and all other manner of animal racket.

This was about as low as it got for a writer.

After all, how could he make use of animal sounds to communicate helpful messages to his nephews? Naturally, preventing this had been the intention of Mr. Shakespeare, who forbade all communication from the Great Beyond down to Earth, considering Mr. Poe the worst offender.

But this latest demotion was not what infuriated Mr. Poe just now.

It was the outrage he observed down on Earth.

How dare that strutting, overblown Professor Perry plan to use one of Mr. Poe's own imaginary inventions (the giant, razor-sharp pendulum from "The Pit and the Pendulum") to inflict *actual* violence on one of the twins?

What was to be done?

Mr. Poe didn't yet know how the professor planned to lure the boys into danger, but there could be no doubt about the man's intentions.

If Mr. Poe still worked in the Fortune Cookie Division, he could have communicated to the twins:

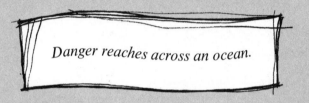

Danger reaches across an ocean.

And if he still worked in the License Plate Division:

And if he were able to steal into Mr. Pablo Picasso's Art Division, as he'd done once before, he'd create a poster-size image of dolls in international attire, all of whom bore the wretched face of Professor Perry, beneath the now ominous phrase, "It's a Small World After All."

But Mr. Picasso would never again allow him entry.

Likewise, Mr. Michelangelo kept him from the Personalized Coffee Mug Division's massive kiln. And Mr. Orville and Mr. Wilbur Wright had long ago barred the hangar doors to the Skywriting Division. All of which left Mr. Poe with the next-to-impossible task of making something useful out of animal sounds.

Moo, baa, neigh, oink . . .

"Blazes!" Mr. Poe cursed aloud.

"Something wrong, Ed?"

Mr. Poe spun around in his desk chair, surprised to find Mr. Walt Whitman, the shaggy-haired poet who'd been dead a mere 120 years or so.

"What are you doing here?" Mr. Poe asked.

"I've just come downstairs for a visit," Mr. Whitman answered gently. "How are your zeal, manliness, and spirit, Ed?"

"My name's Edgar, not Ed," Mr. Poe answered peevishly. They'd been officemates for decades, and Mr. Whitman had never gotten it right.

The poet grinned, his eyes wide and friendly, his mouth almost lost in his unruly white beard.

"Thanks for stopping by, but right now I think I'd rather be alone." Mr. Poe was in no mood for Mr. Whitman's earthy, life-affirming observations. "Why don't you go pay a visit to a barber or something?"

Mr. Whitman laughed. "Your angry wit is exhilarating. It is life!"

Mr. Poe shook his head. "I hate to break the news to you, Walt. But it's not 'life,' seeing as we're both dead."

"True, but isn't that exhilarating too?"

Mr. Poe sighed. This was exactly the kind of optimism that often aggravated him. "Don't you have work to do? Can't you go 'sing your body electric' someplace else?"

Mr. Whitman's eyes grew sympathetic. "Always remember, Ed, you're not alone. You contain multitudes."

Mr. Poe refrained from saying aloud what he thought it was that Mr. Whitman not only contained, but was full of. But then, what could one expect of a poet who didn't even know how to rhyme?

"We've all missed you upstairs," Mr. Whitman said.

"All?" Mr. Poe asked doubtfully.

"Well, OK, maybe not Mr. Shakespeare."

"I was never much good with bosses," Mr. Poe said.

"Me neither," replied Mr. Whitman. "In your conflicts with Mr. Shakespeare, my heart was always with you, Ed."

Mr. Poe studied Mr. Whitman's eyes and found friendship and sympathy there. He was simpatico, as the young Spanish poet Mr. Federico García Lorca, whose cubicle was next to Mr. Whitman's, would say.

"What am I going to do with animal grunts and howls and hisses, Walt?" Mr. Poe asked, revealing more desperation than he'd intended. "How do I communicate anything at all to my nephews?"

Mr. Whitman put his hand on Mr. Poe's shoulder. "'O for the voices of animals!'" the bearded bard of Brooklyn said.

Ordinarily, Mr. Poe wasn't fond of other poets quoting their own work. But Mr. Whitman's line stirred a new idea. "Would you please repeat that?"

Mr. Whitman obliged. "'O for the voices of animals!'"

Yes, that *was* inspired!

"Thanks for coming downstairs," Mr. Poe said to Mr. Whitman, shaking his hand.

Mr. Whitman pulled the handshake into a manly hug.

Mr. Poe found that up close the shaggy poet smelled of freshly mown grass—and a little fertilizer. But he didn't mind, because he was distractedly contemplating a new and ingenious way to connect with the twins. "I've much work to do now," he said, pulling away and turning back to his desk. "After all, achieving the impossible will not be easy."

HAUNTING THE LIBRARY

EDGAR, Allan, and Stevie "The Hulk" Harrison jogged around the corner of Cathedral and Franklin Streets, picking up the pace as they neared the steps to the magisterial main entrance of the Enoch Pratt Free Library, the longtime pride of Baltimore's book lovers. But this was to be no mere browsing session.

The boys had a mission.

"What if they don't have the book you want?" Stevie asked as they started up toward the massive doors.

"No worries," the boys answered.

Surely a library the size of a city block would contain a copy of *The Life and Mysterious Death of Edgar Allan Poe* by Joseph Byron (even if the book had been published close to a century before). Wasn't the twins' great-great-great-great granduncle the city's greatest literary figure?

The trio passed through the pillared arches and tall doors.

"Hey, this place is impressive," Stevie observed, moving into the library's large marble foyer. "It could be a state capitol building." He looked up at the intricately decorated glass ceiling, which cast the subtle, sunlit colors over the foyer.

"Is this the first time you've ever been here?" Allan asked.

Stevie nodded. "I generally use the Internet."

Edgar and Allan didn't have that option, due to Uncle Jack and Aunt Judith's edict. But the twins weren't sure they didn't prefer libraries anyway. They loved the smell of books. And the mazelike possibilities of rows upon rows of tall bookshelves. The Enoch Pratt Free Library was as familiar to them as their home.

"What if somebody's already checked out the book you want?" Stevie asked as they moved past the information and checkout desks toward the grand staircase.

"That's unlikely," Allan said, starting upstairs. "It's not exactly a current best seller."

"Or what if it got lost over all these years?"

"Hey, Stevie, if we'd known you were going to worry so much, we wouldn't have brought you along," Edgar said.

"Oh, I'm not worried," Stevie answered. "Even if the book's not here. I *like* watching you two deal with the unexpected. Like that time Mr. Witt came back into class and found you had taken the magnesium strips and—"

"This is a *library*, Stevie," interrupted Allan. "Organized with the Library of Congress Classification system. What could be unexpected here?"

"I guess you're right."

Actually, the Poe twins knew that the unexpected could happen anywhere, anytime.

"Hey, actually, why *did* you guys bring me along?" Stevie asked. They turned at the top of the stairs and walked past another reference desk toward the biography section, which occupied an entire room.

"Oh, we were just walking by your house on the way here and said to ourselves, 'Wouldn't it be great to hang with Stevie?'" Edgar said.

"My house is not on the way here," Stevie pointed out.

There was a silence.

"OK, we needed somebody big enough to fit Roderick inside his shirt so nobody would notice."

"Oh, great," Stevie said loudly.

The trio turned down a row of bookshelves for privacy.

"Stevie, cats aren't allowed in libraries," Edgar whispered. "And they inspect backpacks."

"And we weren't going to leave Roderick behind," added Allan.

"Meow," Roderick agreed quietly from within Stevie's size XXXL shirt.

"Besides, Stevie, you know it's not just your size. We really do like being with you."

Stevie nodded. The Poe twins often helped him. For example, they'd once arranged an unscheduled series of small rockets to launch on the soccer field *in the middle of a game*. All the players had been distracted except Stevie, who'd been tipped off to the plan, and so he'd scored his only goal of the season, unopposed.

"Well, I'm happy to help in any way I can, I guess. Even if it's as a pet carrier."

"Hey, Roderick's more than just a pet," Edgar reminded him.

"Sure, I know," Stevie said.

The three boys (and cat) passed through an archway and entered another large, Georgian-style room. The biography section began at one end with the baseball player Hank Aaron and ended many, many shelves later with the Persian mystic Zoroaster.

The selection of Edgar Allan Poe biographies occupied almost two whole bookshelves.

"Impressive," Stevie acknowledged as they perused the books, arranged alphabetically by author. "Almost as impressive as having an NFL team named after his most famous poem."

The twins continued scanning the shelves. "Yeah, go Ravens," they muttered.

"Here it is," Allan said. *"The Life and Mysterious Death of Edgar Allan Poe."*

"Does it have the page?" Stevie asked.

Allan flipped to 277. "It's here."

"What's it say?"

Roderick poked his head out of Stevie's shirt, interested in the mysterious text.

The Poe twins read it silently.

"Well?" Stevie pressed.

Allan closed the book and shook his head disappointedly. "It's just an old, discredited claim about the death of our great-great-great-great granduncle."

"What claim?"

"That he was murdered," Edgar answered.

"Murdered by who?" Stevie took the book from Allan's hands, and Roderick examined the pages with him.

Allan's face betrayed his disgust. "According to his jealous literary rivals, the scandalous newspapers of the day, and far too many historians since then, the great Edgar Allan Poe was, essentially, beaten to death."

"By who?"

Edgar answered: "Either by political thugs who mistook him for a common drunk or by the brutish brothers of a woman he was courting at the time."

"Murder?" Stevie again scanned page 277. "Interesting."

"Oh, it's just conjecture," Allan interrupted, taking the book back from his friend and snapping it closed. "The 'murder' theory has been seriously questioned in recent years by many scholars."

"Our great-great-great-great granduncle likely died of a brain disorder or some other natural cause," Edgar added. "Nothing more, nothing less. Just a great loss for humanity."

The three boys and cat were silent. Death was unsettling, however it was served up.

But after a moment, Stevie spoke. "Then why would someone deliver the book to your house just to make sure you noticed that particular page?"

The twins looked at each other. "That's a good question, Stevie," they said.

Suddenly, Stevie's eyes widened and his face went white. "It's—it's—it's *him*!" he stammered, looking past them.

Allan and Edgar turned.

Standing at the end of the long shelf of books, perhaps thirty yards away, was Edgar Allan Poe—the author, poet, dead ancestor. In the non-corporeal flesh!

Real as life.

For once, the twins were almost awed.

They'd learned in New Orleans that this was exactly how ghosts appear. And it was also true that their great-great-great-great granduncle had died within a mile or two of here, well within the circumference allowed for wandering spirits.

"L-L-Look!" Stevie stuttered.

The great author held up one finger, as if asking for a moment of stillness and attention.

How could the twins be anything but attentive?

"Reynolds," the great author said, his voice barely above a whisper.

"Uncle Edgar?" the twins said aloud, starting toward the apparition.

And then the lights went out.

There was total blackness in the biography room.

The twins continued forward, feeling their way along the shelves. But it was to no avail.

When the lights came back on a moment later, the apparition was gone.

"Was that who I think it was?" Stevie sputtered. "Should I believe my own eyes?"

The twins were silent.

"What was that name he said?" Stevie continued. "Reynolds? Who's Reynolds?"

Edgar shook his head. "No one knows, though it's been much considered over the past hundred and sixty-five years."

"Why?"

"Because it was one of the last words our great-great-great-great granduncle said in the hospital before he died," Allan answered.

"He cried it out several times," Edgar added.

"Oh," Stevie said quietly.

"So maybe it *wasn't* a brain disorder," Edgar said.

"He wouldn't be haunting these streets if it had been natural causes or even an accident," Allan agreed.

The twins once more opened the book to page 277.

"It looks like we have another murder to solve," Edgar said, almost to himself.

"Another spirit to set free," Allan added.

Stevie looked around, very nervous. "Who knew the library was such an exciting place?"

WHAT THE POE TWINS DID NOT KNOW . . .
A TYPED NOTE IN A SEALED ENVELOPE SLIPPED THAT AFTERNOON UNDER THE OFFICE DOOR OF M. ALEXANDER MARTIN, PHD, PROFESSOR OF PHYSICS AT JOHNS HOPKINS UNIVERSITY, BALTIMORE, MARYLAND

SUBJECT: PERSONAL

Dear Professor Martin,

First, allow me to congratulate you on your recent article in *Physics Journal*. You are a genius. Your scientific speculations are revolutionary (even if they are *far* less developed than mine, which I have kept secret from the scientific community). Having said that, I'm afraid I have some bad news for you . . . there's not room for the two of us in this world.

Let me explain.

Your article concerns quantum entanglement—the theory that a pair of subatomic particles separated from one another, even by distances as wide as the whole universe, may remain tied together in a mysterious fashion. The two particles act as one, instantaneously responding to each other. Of course, all this is elementary, but in your article you ask what might occur if objects larger than mere particles were "entangled."

Well, I have indeed discovered something larger than mere particles—*human beings*, identical twin boys whose linked minds somehow defy space and time. You and I know the long odds against such an occurrence. But that is why *my* work cannot be threatened by your scribblings. You see, I plan to kill one of the twins while imprisoning the other, which will enable me to use the captive as a human channel to contact his brother in the afterlife, resulting in unimagined access to information and worldly power!

Now do you see why I can't allow another physicist to speculate publicly about "large-object quantum entanglement"? Do you understand how threatening public attention could be? Do you acknowledge that this world just isn't big enough for the two of us? And, finally, do you grasp why I planted beneath your desk a small explosive, activated a moment ago when you opened the envelope that contained this letter?

Sincerely,

Professor P.

P.S. That's right, 3-2-1 . . . *BANG!*

REYNOLDS WHO?

AFTER returning home, Edgar and Allan said very little over dinner. A tale of the ghost of Edgar Allan Poe haunting the stacks of the Enoch Pratt Free Library would elicit disbelief on Uncle Jack's face and barely contained terror on Aunt Judith's. Why burden them? Besides, Uncle Jack was full of NFL playoff talk, and Aunt Judith was anxious to discuss the latest entertainment news. The twins didn't exactly ignore them, but responded with agreeable and benign answers that took no thought.

"You're right, Uncle Jack, we could win the Super Bowl this year."

"You're right, Aunt Judith, that new movie star is sure behaving irresponsibly."

Meantime, these more pressing questions were what actually occupied the twins' shared thoughts:

Q. If Edgar Allan Poe *had* been murdered, then why had he waited so long to make himself known to the twins, who'd lived their whole lives in downtown Baltimore, the general area of his demise?

A. Perhaps Edgar and Allan were of use to the great author only now, *after* meeting the Du Valiers in New Orleans and coming to understand how things worked with murdered souls.

Q. Why had their great-great-great-great granduncle not spoken more to them in the library?

A. Just because some spirits were chatty didn't necessarily mean *all* of them were capable of talking up a storm.

Q. While spirits can materialize and speak, they aren't capable of moving physical objects. So who had delivered the book with the missing page that led to the boys' meeting the spirit in the library?

A. Perhaps the spirit of the great author had communicated instructions to a human agent who was too terrified to stick around long enough to identify him- or herself.

Q. How were the twins to solve Poe's murder when their great-great-great-great granduncle had offered only a clue already long known to history: the name Reynolds?

A: ???

"Boys, you're dripping marinara sauce!" Aunt Judith exclaimed, reaching to wipe at the red splotches on the tablecloth.

The twins snapped out of their shared trance.

"Whoops," they said, dabbing at their shirts with their napkins. It looked as if someone had been murdered right there at the dinner table.

"What a mess." Their uncle tutted.

With so many good questions and so few good answers, it seemed to Edgar and Allan that Uncle Jack had *no idea* what a real mess was.

Fortunately, the Poe twins liked it when things got messy.

That night, Edgar and Allan stayed up very late.

Actually, they didn't sleep at all.

It was not the otherworldly sighting itself that kept them awake. They had experienced that in New Orleans, along with Em and Milly Dickinson. It was the boys' burning desire to solve their legendary forebear's murder to set him free from haunting the vicinity of the horrible crime.

But they had only one clue.

Reynolds.

The boys lay on their backs in their twin beds staring distractedly at the cracks in the ceiling as they ran through their encyclopedic knowledge.

"It can't be an allusion to the R. J. Reynolds Tobacco Company," Edgar whispered.

Allan concurred. "That wasn't founded until decades after our great-uncle's death. And the Reynolds Metals Company was founded even later."

"Right, which rules out tobacco or metallurgy."

"Both potential causes of illness. But for our purposes—useless."

Roderick had gone to sleep on his satin cushion, preferring dreams of catnip and field mice to listening to the twins' speculations.

"And it's not an allusion to astronomy, specifically the Hubble-Reynolds Law," Edgar continued.

$$I(R) = \frac{I_0}{(1 + R/R_H)^2}$$

Being an expression of the surface brightness of elliptical galaxies, this was one of the Poe twins' favorite astronomical laws. But what good did it do them now?

"And as for individuals who lived in that era . . ." Allan considered.

They started with the obvious choice. "Of course, there's Jeremiah Reynolds," Edgar said.

Jeremiah Reynolds was a newspaper editor who thought the Earth was hollow. That belief, and Reynolds's sailing trip to Antarctica, had inspired Edgar Allan Poe's novel, *The Narrative of Arthur Gordon Pym of Nantucket*.

"But why would Jeremiah Reynolds commit murder?" Allan objected. "Poe supported his unusual beliefs. So where's the motive?"

Edgar agreed. "How about Alexander Reynolds, the American general?"

"He attended West Point," Allan said.

They shared a lightning-fast calculation.

Allan said, with frustration, "Drat. That was two years *after* our great-uncle had been expelled, so they'd never have met."

The boys sighed.

"What if he meant a fictional person, not a real one?" Edgar proposed. "Like Mrs. Reynolds, the housekeeper in Jane Austen's novel *Pride and Prejudice*."

"Our great-uncle likely read it."

"And while a fictional character can't commit a real murder, maybe the ghost was alluding to an actual housekeeper," Edgar continued, sitting up in bed. "Maybe the housekeeper did it!"

"But our great-uncle could never afford to employ a housekeeper."

"That's true," Edgar acknowledged, his enthusiasm fading as he fell back to the mattress. "Nor did any friends, acquaintances, or members of his family work as housekeepers."

"Drat!" Allan said again.

Suddenly, the door to the boys' bedroom burst open.

Uncle Jack's silhouette filled the doorway. He stepped into the moonlit room, his eyes sleepy and his body lumpy and disheveled in striped pajamas. "Do you two have any idea *what time it is*?" he snapped.

The twins hadn't realized that in their enthusiasm they'd raised their voices.

"*Well?*"

Edgar glanced at the clock on the night table. "It's 2:44 a.m., Uncle Jack," he said matter-of-factly.

Allan rolled onto one elbow, facing his uncle. "Wouldn't it have been simpler for you to just look at your own clock rather than come in here if you wanted to know the time?"

"Quiet down and go to sleep!" Uncle Jack ordered. He slammed the door after him.

Roderick awoke and looked at the door with a disgruntled expression.

So much for quiet.

The twins waited for Uncle's Jack's footsteps to recede down the hall before they began whispering again.

More possibilities, more conjecture.

The boys brimmed with Reynolds references and allusions, Reynoldses fictional and actual, Reynolds, Reynolds, Reynolds . . .

It was nearly as difficult as figuring out the nine-digit code to the Bradbury Telecommunications Satellite's remote navigational system. And they hadn't solved that yet either.

When daylight brightened their window and the alarm clock went off at seven a.m., they'd come up with nothing useful.

Once again, their bedroom door opened.

"Rise and shine, boys!" Aunt Judith said, smiling in her housecoat and hair curlers.

The twins rose.

But they weren't exactly shining.

☙ ☠ ❧

Allan and Edgar were only half awake when they arrived at their adjacent lockers before first period. They spun through their identical combinations, opening the metal doors and placing their lunch sacks atop their stacked textbooks.

Slam! went the metal doors.

"Can you guys believe what we saw yesterday at the library?" called Stevie "The Hulk" from across the hallway.

Edgar and Allan shot him withering glares. They'd asked him to keep it to himself.

"What did you guys see?" asked David Litke, who'd overheard and had come now to stand beside Stevie.

Stevie lowered his eyes as he noted the twins' glares

and realized what he'd done. He turned from them to David. "Oh, um, nothing," he said unconvincingly.

David looked at him questioningly. Then he turned to the twins. "Are you leaving me out of something?"

"Would we do that?" the twins answered.

"That's what I'm asking you."

"What kind of friends would that make us?" Edgar responded.

"The kind who keep secrets," David answered bluntly.

"Exactly," Allan said. "And what kind of friend is that?"

David considered. "Oh . . . OK," he responded, half-satisfied, half-confused. Then he wandered into the morning crowd.

The twins hadn't lied to him. They'd just answered his questions with other questions until he provided for himself the answer *he* was looking for. This was a ruse Edgar and Allan usually employed only with adults. But this morning they were tired and discouraged and didn't want to explain what was likely to come next—that the ghost of Edgar Allan Poe had offered a clue from which the twins had, as yet, managed to discern . . . *nothing*.

"Sorry," Stevie whispered when David moved away. "I'll keep it to myself, like we said."

"There'll be a proper time for us to share it with everybody," Allan answered.

The bell rang, and the boys made their way to Mrs. Rosecrans's classroom, where they took their seats without further incident.

"Good morning, class," she said.

Then she began to talk about the public speaking exercise from the week before. The twins weren't much interested—at least, not until she said, "And Miss Reynolds, who is a real expert, told me in an e-mail that she thinks there are some potentially outstanding orators in this room."

The twins' hands darted immediately into the air. "Miss *who?* Did you say *Reynolds?*"

Mrs. Rosecrans smiled. "Ah, I forgot. Yes, she insisted on you children calling her by her first name, Birdy. I can't say I approve of such informality, but it was her choice."

"Miss Reynolds?" Edgar cried.

Classmates turned to him, confused by his enthusiasm.

"Yes," Mrs. Rosecrans said cautiously.

The Poe twins turned to each other.

Could it be a coincidence?

Edgar and Allan didn't believe in coincidence. "We

have some questions for you about Miss Reynolds," they said.

Mrs. Rosecrans smiled. "Well, I'm glad to see you two taking such interest in public speaking."

"How do you know her?" Edgar asked.

"Where does she live?" Allan asked.

"Where does she work?" Edgar asked.

"Does she seem like the type to keep secrets?" Allan asked.

"About murders and such," Edgar elaborated.

Mrs. Rosecrans held up her hand like a traffic cop. "Murders?" She was clearly dismayed. "You boys are completely out of hand. Miss Reynolds is a respectable woman."

"Oh, we don't mean *she* committed murder, but—" Allan started.

"That's enough!" Mrs. Rosecrans snapped.

The twins quieted, wondering what had become of the sympathetic woman of the week before.

Their teacher gathered herself and straightened at the podium. "If you two have questions about Miss Reynolds, you may ask me after class," she said.

WHAT THE POE TWINS DID NOT KNOW . . .

BALTIMORE SUN

All the News That Print Can Fit

PHYSICS PROFESSOR MURDERED

Baltimore, MD—M. Alexander Martin, PhD, a longtime physics professor at Johns Hopkins University, was fatally injured in a bombing at his office yesterday at approximately 9:25 a.m. The department secretary, Elsie Franklin, reported that Professor Martin was opening his morning mail at the time of the explosion.

While the cause of death cannot be officially confirmed until after an autopsy, campus police chief J. P. Knapp said, "It seems pretty obvious what happened here, though who committed the crime remains a mystery."

As to motive, both colleagues and law enforcement agencies are confounded, as Professor Martin was well-liked on campus.

Pictured above: Professor M. A. Martin delivering a lecture.

LOOK AT THE BIRDY

AFTER class, the twins peppered Mrs. Rosecrans with questions.

Her answers were earnest and useful, even if they were frustrating. She and Birdy Reynolds knew each other only from the weekly Roastmasters meetings they both attended at the Bayside Motor Inn on Fridays at six a.m. (an hour chosen to allow participants to make it to their jobs on time).

"*Every* Friday?" Edgar asked impatiently, wishing this were Thursday instead of Tuesday.

Mrs. Rosecrans nodded. "A couple of weeks ago, after I gave a short speech about my teaching career, Miss Reynolds introduced herself and offered to visit my class to discuss public speaking. And that's all I know about her. Of course, I *might* have learned more, since she and

I had planned to have coffee after class in the teachers' lounge, but your speech about ghosts scared her clean off the campus."

"But she'll be at this Friday's Roastmasters meeting?" Allan asked.

"I presume," answered Mrs. Rosecrans.

"Are children allowed at the meetings?" inquired Edgar.

She nodded. "You two can come, *if* you're willing to give a talk of some kind."

Talking was no problem for the twins. "We'll be there," they answered.

"And not just some speech off the tops of your heads," Mrs. Rosecrans added. "Something planned."

"Oh, we'll have a plan," they assured her.

☙ ☠ ❧

On Friday morning, Edgar strolled alone into the Roastmasters meeting as if there was nothing unusual about his being there. Wasn't he attired in a suit and tie, just like the businessmen who milled about the room? And didn't he carry himself with confidence, making small talk with many of the well-coiffed businesswomen who placed their designer purses on folding chairs to save the best seats for themselves? So what if Edgar was the only person under eighteen in the room? A few minutes earlier, he, Allan, Stevie "The Hulk," and Katie Justus (with whom they'd shared the news of the ghostly Poe sighting) had been the only people under eighteen on the city bus ride—and that had been no problem.

"Excellent polish job on those wing-tip shoes, sir," Edgar said to a gray-haired man in a three-piece suit.

Meantime, Stevie, Katie, and Allan took their secret positions behind a large stainless steel cabinet in the empty kitchen adjacent to the meeting room. Each wore a nineteenth century–style costume "borrowed" from Aldrin Middle School's drama department. Additionally, Allan sported a small false mustache in the style of his famous ancestor.

They awaited their cue.

Back in the meeting room, the Roastmasters—their cups of coffee held before them in two hands, like sacred objects—seemed glad to welcome Edgar.

That is, all but Mrs. Rosecrans, who gave a quick but fretful smile from across the room. The Poe twins, as she well knew, were always unpredictable. But she *had* agreed to let them deliver a speech here as extra credit for the Shakespeare unit in English class. So what could she do now but cross her fingers?

Edgar was really only concerned with one person: Miss Birdy Reynolds.

And there she was!

"Hello, Birdy," Edgar called as he crossed the room. She turned to him. "Your visit to our class inspired me to pursue public speaking more seriously. So I'm here to be a Roastmaster."

Birdy Reynolds smiled. "Welcome, young man," she said, straightening nonexistent wrinkles in her stylish Chanel suit.

"Is there a sign-up sheet for speaking?" Edgar asked.

"Oh, we'll make an exception for you," she answered. "We like to encourage youthful enthusiasm. In fact, you can go first."

"Thanks. I think you'll be very interested in my topic."

"May I ask what it is?"

"Murder," he said.

Birdy Reynolds gasped.

"Oh, not a recent murder," Edgar added reassuringly. "One dating all the way back to 1849."

She stood up straighter.

"Do *you* happen to know anything about a murder in 1849?" Edgar asked pointedly.

She said nothing. Likewise, her expression betrayed nothing.

"If you come clean now it'll save us time and trouble," Edgar whispered.

Birdy Reynolds seemed just about to cooperate when Mrs. Rosecrans joined them. "Good morning, fellow Roastmasters," Mrs. Rosecrans said to Birdy Reynolds with what seemed to Edgar artificial cheer. Then she turned to him, her voice tinged with suspicion. "What's the plan here, Edgar?"

The plan was to employ a trick from William Shakespeare's *Hamlet*, wherein Prince Hamlet puts on a play that recreates a recent murder in order to observe how the presumed killer will react. All the innocent audience members think it's merely a story, but the guilty party recognizes it for what it is—an accusation— and the killer's panic betrays his guilt.

"May I have your attention?" came a voice over the PA system, interrupting all the chatter in the room. Edgar turned and saw a white-haired man at the podium. "If you'll all get seated, we can get started."

The perfumed ladies rejoined their designer purses at their seats, and the business-suited men settled into those that were left over. A hush replaced the chattering of a moment before.

Edgar didn't bother finding a chair but started straight for the podium.

"Ah, I see we have our first speaker," the white-haired man said. "And, even better, it's a youngster. We at Roastmasters appreciate youngsters. Welcome, youngster." He chuckled and patted Edgar on top of the head.

"Youngster"—what a ridiculous word, thought Edgar. He patiently waited for the man to take his seat with the others.

Then he began. "Ladies and gentlemen, my name is Edgar Poe, and I'm pleased to join you in this lovely meeting room to talk of a crime long unsolved. Nay, to do more than merely talk of it, but to dramatize it. Nay, more than that, to solve it! If you please, imagine this fair city in the year 1849, alive with a thriving seaport and citizens both respectable and disreputable. Passing among them happens to be Baltimore's most venerable literary figure, the great Edgar Allan Poe."

At this, the swinging double doors to the kitchen

burst open and the costumed Allan stumbled into the room, crying aloud: "I've been beaten, kicked, bruised! O why, when I am so undeserving of violence? My life force . . . it is slipping away."

All the Roastmasters turned wide-eyed in their chairs toward the unexpected commotion.

Allan stumbled farther into the room, his face streaming fake blood. "Who has done this dire deed to me?" he cried, before falling "dead" at the base of the podium.

The Roastmasters looked at one another, dumb-founded.

Then the kitchen doors opened again, and nineteenth-century versions of Stevie and Katie raced into the meeting room, tracing Allan's path.

"What vile villain has done this to such a great man?" cried Stevie in a booming voice. "Poe, the greatest of all American writers, dead!"

"It is Reynolds who did it!" said Katie, who had played Cosette in Aldrin Middle School's production of *Les Misérables*. "Reynolds is the murderer!"

Stevie and Katie knelt brokenheartedly beside the body of the great Poe, while Edgar leaned from the podium to loom over the scene, speaking in as deep a register as he could muster, like a voice from the heavens: "Shall we let this crime go unsolved?"

After a moment of silence, he straightened and said in his regular voice to the audience, "Thank you, Roastmasters, for your rapt attention."

The Roastmasters looked confused. All except one member: Miss Birdy Reynolds.

She was weeping in her seat.

The plan had worked!

The white-haired man rejoined Edgar at the podium. "Thank you," he said, a bit baffled, "for your dramatization."

There was a spattering of applause.

Edgar joined his brother and friends in front of the podium, where they bowed as one.

Mrs. Rosecrans looked perturbed.

Miss Birdy Reynolds indicated for Edgar and Allan to come to meet her near the coffee urn at the back of the room.

Would she reprimand them? Threaten them? Deny everything?

They met. "Thank you, boys," she said.

Edgar and Allan were taken aback.

"I've lived with the secret of your ancestor's murder for far too long," she said with feeling. "The whole Reynolds family, generation after generation . . . secrets eat at the heart. It's time I share the truth about what my ancestor did to yours."

The twins glowed, on the verge of solving another ancient murder and setting another ghost free!

"Which ancestor?" Allan asked.

"And why'd he do it?" Edgar added.

She shook her head. "I'll share the story *exclusively* with you two and your family," she continued. "Poes only. What you do with it afterward, the newspapers, television, the Internet . . . it's up to you." She handed Edgar a printed calling card with her name and address.

Miss Birdy Reynolds
Willowtree Manor
Green Spring Valley, MD

"Tomorrow night, at my estate," she continued. "I'll send a limousine for you and yours at seven. Then dinner. And truth."

And justice, the boys thought.

They gave her their address.

Then Miss Birdy Reynolds turned and fled the room.

"What kind of English project was that?" Mrs. Rosecrans demanded as she caught up to the boys.

"An A-plus," they answered.

WHAT THE POE TWINS DID NOT KNOW . . .

CODED NOTES FOR PROFESSOR S. PANGBORN PERRY'S
AUTOBIOGRAPHY, JOTTED IN A SECOND-STORY ROOM
OF A GREEN SPRING VALLEY MANSION:

⊹✳⊹℧ℛⓄ ℍ℧ ⌂L⊹℧ ℧∇ℛ ℒℚ△∇℧ ⓄⓍⓄℛⵁ℧⤬

♂ℚ℧∇ ℧∇ℛ ∇ℛⵗⵠ⋌ ⤫⊊ Ⓞ✳ ℍℨ℧ℒℛ⊹⊹

⊹ℒℚℤℛⵁ✳ ℚⵁ ℧∇ℛ ℒⵣℤℛ ⤫⊊ ⊞ℚ⊹⊹ Ⓞℚℒ✳✳

ℼℛ✳ⵁⵗⵠ⊹⊊𝒞 ᚖℚℤ∇ ℧∇ℛ ℛⵠℚⓄℚⵁℍ℧ℚⵗ∅

⤫⊊ Ⓞ✳ ⵗⵁⵠ✳ ⊹ℨ∇⤫ⵠℍℒⵣ✳ ℒℚⵤℍⵠ𝒞

ⵠℒⵗ⤫ℛ⊹⊹⤫ℒℬ ⊞ℍℒ℧ℚⵁ∅𝒞 ℍⵁ✚ ᚖℚ℧∇ Ⓞ✳

ℼⵗⵁℼⵗℨℼ℧ℚⵗ∅ ⤫⊊ ℍ ℧ℍ⊹℧ℛⵣℛ⊹⊹𝒞

⤫⊹⤫ℒⵣⵠℛ⊹⊹ ∇⵿⤫ℼ∇⤫Lℰ ⊹ℒL△ ⊹⤫ℒ ℛℍℼ∇

ⓄℛⓄⓄℛℒ ⤫⊊ ℧∇ℛ ⵠ⤫ℛ ⊹ℍⓄⵣⵠ✳𝒞 𝓂 ⵁ⤫ℯ

ℍⵠⵠℒ⤫ℍℼ∇ ℧∇ℛ ℼLⵠⓄℚⵁℍ℧ℚⵗ∅ ⤫⊊ Ⓞ∴

ⵠℚⵗℛ’⊹ ᚖ⤫ℒ∇✳

NOTE: The text of the preceding letter is written in a replacement code intended to disguise the communication as mere gibberish. The decoded translation is as follows:

While pretending to be unconscious in my hospital bed in Kansas (before escaping from the local police), I took some time to consider my failure back at the Dorothy Gale Farm and OZitorium. Just how had those brats eluded me? A lesser man might have avoided such a painful question. But I am not a lesser man.

If the ever-connected Poe twins are to be mine,

then I must draw from the same inspiration that animates them: their ancestor Edgar Allan Poe. My previous inspiration, Professor Marvel from *The Wizard of Oz*, failed to provide me with sufficient malice to overcome the twins, who, after all, are descended from a man of truly dark imagination. A wicked witch and flying monkeys are mere child's play when compared to the horrors found in Poe's stories. Lying in my hospital bed, I realized I had to turn the twins' own ancestor's imagination against them. Yes, the pendulum swings!

With this thought foremost, I've made my way to the boys' hometown from Shanghai, where Dr. Psufo performed surgical magic and gave me a famous new face.

I am a whirlwind of vengeance and ambition, for whom impersonating the ghost of a long-dead literary genius is no more difficult than using a tiny handheld device to short out a library's electrical system at just the right moment. With the help of my actress friend in the role of Miss Birdy Reynolds, with the elimination of my only scholarly rival, Professor Martin, and with my concoction of a tasteless, odorless knockout drug for each member of the Poe family, I now approach the culmination of my life's work!

Mr Poe in the Great Beyond

Sitting at his desk, Mr. Poe muttered, "How dare that strutting villain disguise himself as the ghost of *me*!"

Of all people!

With the plastic surgery and hairpiece that Perry had obtained while hiding in Shanghai, he *was* virtually indistinguishable from Mr. Poe's famous portrait photograph of 1840. Indeed, Edgar and Allan had already been fooled into believing that their great-great-great-great granduncle had been murdered. In truth, the great author had died of a brain tumor—a natural cause of death—which was, of course, why he was here rather than haunting Baltimore.

And events on Earth seemed to be growing only worse!

Soon, the twins would take a limousine ride to an

isolated country estate. What terrors awaited them there?

Mr. Poe feared he knew: the pendulum.

But he wasn't beaten yet. He'd been hard at work.

"Mr. Poe?"

A soft, female voice. He spun his chair around.

"Ah, Miss Dickinson," he said, standing up to greet her formally.

He had not seen her since his demotion. Until now, only Mr. Whitman had taken the elevator ride down to the clamorous barnyard on the 121,347,935th floor for a social call.

"It's gracious of you to call on me," he said, straightening his cravat.

Miss Emily Dickinson was as lovely, demure, and well-kept as always, her complexion creamy from so little exposure to the sun during her lifetime, her hair in a neat bun, her black dress modest and without a wrinkle. At first glance, she might have been mistaken for an ordinary woman. But the light in her eyes indicated that there was nothing ordinary about her—she was a poet of enormous courage, power, and depth, perhaps the second best of the nineteenth century, by Mr. Poe's estimation.

"I wish I had a plate of crumpets and a pot of tea to offer you," Mr. Poe continued. "But I'm a little out of sorts just now."

She waved away his apology. "I didn't come here to drink tea, but to see you."

Mr. Poe's heart beat a little faster. "How are your lovely great-great-great-great grandnieces?"

"Em and Milly are well," she answered. "Their travels in Mexico and Central America have been rich with new experiences." She hesitated. "I'm told that travel does that."

"Yes," Mr. Poe said. He knew that in Miss Dickinson's entire lifetime she had barely left her house, let alone her hometown of Amherst. Her travel had been limited to the universe in a human heart.

"The girls will be returning soon to Baltimore," she said. "And how are your nephews?"

"Ah, Edgar and Allan," Mr. Poe said. "Actually, they're in grave danger."

"I'm so sorry to hear it."

"Oh, I've not taken it lying down. There's no 'give up' in Edgar Allan Poe. I believe I've come up with a way to help them. As a matter of fact, the timing of your visit couldn't be more auspicious, as I've arranged for a test of my new idea, which is ready to commence just about now."

She looked interested.

"Come with me," he said, striding past her. As they crossed the vast room, which more closely resembled a menagerie than an office, Mr. Poe explained the dire situation facing his great-great-great-great grandnephews. Next, he explained the challenge of communicating to the twins a warning about Professor Perry's deceitful Poe impersonation, upon which all the subsequent lies rested.

"And you've managed to compose such a warning using only animal sounds?" Miss Dickinson asked, impressed.

Mr. Poe nodded as he led the way into a large conference room occupied by a dodo bird, an ox, two snakes, a great egret, a peacock, and a crow. "Thank you all for coming," he said to the animals.

Miss Dickinson's eyes widened.

"I had quite a bit of trouble with English," Mr.

Poe said to his fellow poet. "Fortunately, my great-great-great-great grandnephews are fluent in Latin." He turned to the animals. "Now, get into your proper order, please."

The animals shuffled and slithered into different places, coming into a straight line.

"Naturally, a whole sentence is impossible," Mr. Poe explained to Miss Dickinson. "But the Latin phrase '*dolosa esca*,' which, as you know, means 'deceitful bait,' ought to be sufficient to warn the twins of the professor's disguise."

"*Dolosa esca*?" Miss Dickinson looked confused. "You can get these creatures to speak Latin?"

"Just watch," Mr. Poe said, turning to the animals.

Like a symphony conductor, he raised one hand to quiet them.

Then he pointed to the dodo bird, which made its natural sound: "Doe."

Next, he pointed to the ox, which lowed.

The snake hissed.

The great egret came next. "Ah."

The peacock squawked "Eh."

The second snake hissed.

And the crow screamed: "Kaa!"

Taken together, it sounded like this: *Doe-low-sss-ah / eh-sss-kaa.*

"See, Miss Dickinson?" Mr. Poe said enthusiastically. "*Dolosa esca!* Latin for 'deceitful bait'!"

Miss Dickinson's eyes were even wider than before. "'Great is language ... it is the mightiest of the sciences.'"

Mr. Poe didn't even mind that she was quoting Mr. Whitman's poetry rather than his own.

"It's genius, Mr. Poe."

"Yes, genius is the right word," he said. "But I can't take all the credit." He turned to his animal chorus. "Good work, ladies and gentlemen ... er, I mean, colleagues."

The peacock preened.

"But doesn't *dolosa esca* also mean 'deceitful food'?" asked Miss Dickinson, whose education had been informal but comprehensive.

"Exactly," Mr. Poe answered, grinning. "Which *also* works, since Professor Perry has been experimenting with various forms of tasteless and odorless anesthetics, suggesting he's planning at some point to drug the twins' food. *Dolosa esca* . . . deceitful bait, deceitful food, two warnings in one!"

Miss Dickinson looked impressed. But after a moment, a shadow crossed her face. "But the dodo bird," she said, pointing to the squat, large-billed avian.

"What about it?" asked Mr. Poe.

"It's extinct on Earth."

Mr. Poe slapped his forehead with his palm. "How could I forget?"

Miss Dickinson patted his shoulder. "Being up here makes one forget such things," she said soothingly. "Up here, where nothing and no one is ever extinct."

"That's no excuse," groaned Mr. Poe, deflating with discouragement. "Ah, this ruins everything," he whispered to himself dejectedly. "There's no substitute here for that first syllable."

His animal chorus looked at him sympathetically,

especially the dodo. Even the hyenas in the next room ceased their laughing.

"Why not just deliver the message with a parrot or myna or parakeet or . . . a raven, as in that famous poem of yours?" Miss Dickinson asked reasonably. "Couldn't a talking bird be trained to say '*dolosa esca*' or some other, even more specific warning, in English?"

Mr. Poe shook his head, dejected. "I tried that. But it doesn't work."

"Why not?"

"For some reason, I can only train the talking birds here to speak one word."

"What word?"

"'Nevermore,'" he answered. It was the word spoken by the raven in Mr. Poe's most famous poem. "I'm beaten."

Miss Dickinson put her hand on his shoulder and this time quoted herself:

"'Hope' is the thing with feathers—
That perches in the soul—
And sings the tune without the words—
And never stops—at all—"

Mr. Poe said nothing.

"I have an idea that might be helpful," she said. "In *my* division. Greeting cards."

"You would take that risk?" he asked, surprised.

"The key," she continued, drawing nearer so that she could lower her voice even more, "is to deliver a greeting card that contains a warning subtle enough to escape the attention of Mr. Shakespeare, while still communicating the necessary warning to your rather brilliant nephews."

"Indeed," Mr. Poe agreed. "But there's so little time."

"I'd be honored to use a quote from one of your fine poems or stories. May I?" she asked.

"Of course. Do you have one in mind?"

"Not yet, but I'll find something." She turned and started swiftly toward the elevator.

What a woman! thought Mr. Poe.

O'ER HILL AND DALE

A soft snow was falling as the long black limousine pulled up to the Poe family's house.

Edgar and Allan had been watching for the car.

Now they turned from the living room window and called, "It's here!"

Wiping cookie crumbs from his hands, Uncle Jack came out of the kitchen in his blue suit and best silk tie; meantime, Aunt Judith preened with last-minute intensity in front of the hall mirror. She was dressed in her Sunday best, including the pearls that had come to her through many generations of Poes.

"Let's get a move on," Uncle Jack called to her.

"Just a minute, dear," she answered, making minute adjustments to her already perfect hairstyle. "One doesn't get invited just any old evening to dinner at a hundred-acre private estate in Green Spring Valley. Getting one's appearance right is important."

Roderick stretched, as if to show off his new Italian leather collar.

The twins wore suits but no ties. They wanted to maintain the rough-and-ready appearance of private detectives rather than the appearance of junior business executives.

After all, they *were* detectives.

Edgar carried a digital recorder to get Miss Reynolds's words down for posterity—the solution to a 165-year-old murder mystery that would set free the ghost of their great-great-great-great granduncle.

Naturally, this was reason enough to solve the crime.

But naming the killer of such a famous author would also make global headlines, creating a welcome distraction from the current lead news: the imminent reentry of the Bradbury Telecommunications Satellite.

Newspapers, websites, twenty-four-hour TV news channels . . . There had been predictions of crash landings anywhere from California to Siberia to South Africa. The satellite had been the last place Mal and Irma Poe had been alive. Truth be told, Edgar and Allan felt somehow guilty for the damage the crash might do. All the reassurances of their aunt and uncle failed to make the boys feel otherwise.

This made publicly solving Edgar Allan Poe's murder that much more important.

The doorbell rang.

"Poe family?" the formally clad chauffeur asked as Uncle Jack opened the front door.

Moments later, the four Poes and Roderick settled into the comfortable leather seats in the back of the stretch limousine, which pulled away from their house with a smooth swoosh. This wasn't the first time the boys had ridden in high style. Just a few weeks before, they'd been picked up by limos for their respective TV show appearances in New Orleans. But they'd never been in one this luxurious before. The interior had tiny glittering lights, like a nightclub.

"Look, imported water," Aunt Judith said, taking a small glass bottle from one of the cup holders.

Allan took a bottle too, pouring its bubbling contents into a glass for Roderick, who'd settled comfortably on the thickly carpeted floor.

"And over here, free booze," said Uncle Jack. He didn't drink hard liquor, but he took the top off the crystal decanter and smelled the alcohol anyway. "I think it's the real stuff, from Scotland. We're traveling in *style*, boys."

"And reading lights, like in an airplane," Aunt Judith added, switching on the light above her head. "And free reading material."

Tucked into a leather pouch were a half dozen current magazines along with the day's newspaper, neatly folded.

"They got any news magazines in there?" Uncle Jack asked.

Allan rummaged through. "Here you go, Uncle Jack,"

he said, handing him a magazine with the president of the United States on the cover.

"Thanks," Uncle Jack said, switching on his overhead light.

"Anything for me?" Aunt Judith inquired.

Edgar handed her a glossy magazine about historic homes.

"Perfect," she said.

"And you, Roderick?" Allan asked.

The cat merely purred in response.

"He's all caught up with his reading," Edgar said.

During the forty-five-minute drive to the estate, Allan rummaged through the leather pouch, avoiding the day's newspaper with its satellite speculation, and chose instead a science magazine, which featured articles on turtle eggs and cold fusion energy. Meantime, Edgar leafed through *National Geographic*, taking particular interest in photographs of recently discovered cave paintings in France believed to date back over forty thousand years. With all the reading lights switched on, the family saw only their own reflections in the tinted windows and nothing of the moonlit, snowy night passing at sixty-five miles per hour outside.

The chauffeur turned on the intercom and announced that they were nearing their destination. The Poe family switched off their reading lights to look outside. Moonlight reflected off the newly fallen snow, illuminating skeletal poplar, oak, and maple trees that stretched into a distance of gently rolling hills.

"Beautiful country," Uncle Jack commented.

The limousine slowed to a stop. The chauffeur rolled down the divider that separated the front seat from the passenger section. "This is the gate to the estate," he said. "It's another half mile from here, through the grounds, to the main house."

With the divider down, the Poes could see through the windshield as tall gates slowly parted before them. Then the chauffeur rolled up the divider, obscuring the road ahead as he accelerated through the entrance and onto a gravel road.

Aunt Judith checked her makeup in a compact mirror.

Uncle Jack gathered up the magazines, folded the newspaper, and put them all back into their leather pouch. "Hey," he said, surprised.

"What?" the twins inquired.

Uncle Jack turned to them, switching his reading light back on. "You guys missed these in here." He held two greeting card–size envelopes.

The boys flipped on their reading lights.

Each envelope had been addressed in a beautiful hand:

Edgar and Allan were impressed both by the penmanship and by the formal address: young *masters* . . . It had a nice ring to it, even if Master This-or-That seemed to belong more to the nineteenth century or early twentieth than to today.

"We missed these?" Allan asked his uncle doubtfully.

"Well, they didn't come from nowhere," Uncle Jack replied.

"Are they from you and Aunt Judith?"

The two shook their heads.

"Must be from Miss Reynolds," Aunt Judith suggested. "To welcome you boys to her estate."

It was a reasonable proposition.

Except that the twins were sure the envelopes hadn't been there forty minutes before, when they'd sorted through the magazines.

So where had they come from? And how did they get here?

The boys didn't know.

But they had strong suspicions as to what they were: more cryptic messages from that mysterious entity who for years had been sending them warnings.

"Well, open them," Aunt Judith said, switching on her light.

The twins opened the envelopes and removed identical greeting cards. On the front of each was a picture of a river winding through a northern Italian city that looked familiar, though they couldn't quite place it. And stranger yet was what was written inside:

Thus it appeared, I say, but was not. It was my antagonist . . . not a line in all the marked and singular lineaments of his face which was not, even in the most absolute identity, mine own!

The cards were not signed.

"What the heck?" exclaimed Uncle Jack.

"It's nonsense," said Aunt Judith. "Some kind of prank?"

"Actually, it's excerpted from a short story," Edgar told her. "'William Wilson' by Edgar Allan Poe."

"Is that the one about the man who's shadowed everywhere by his double?" Uncle Jack asked, being more acquainted with his ancestor's work than that of any other writer.

"Right, a doppelgänger," Edgar said.

"A what?" Uncle Jack asked.

"It's a literary term from German," Allan answered. "From *doppel,* meaning 'double,' and *gänger,* meaning 'goer.'"

"Yes, but what about the quote?" Aunt Judith asked.

The twins' singular mind set to work on the problem. And they'd likely have figured it out in a flash . . .

But the limousine made a gentle stop and the back door was opened, not by the chauffeur or even a butler, but by Miss Birdy Reynolds herself, who leaned into the car and said with a smile, "Welcome to my home, dear Poes."

The family piled out into the crisp January night.

"It's too cold to linger here," Miss Reynolds continued. "Come inside."

But the Poes needed a moment to take in the mansion, which was like something out of a strange dream, being a massive amalgam of architectural styles from different historical eras.

The broad marble staircase that led up from the driveway was decorated with golden, Second Empire–style lamps—countless ornate curlicues—like those on some of the bridges in Paris; the fifteen-foot-high wooden front doors at the top of the stairs were made of cross-hatched planks of pine, like the gates of a frontier fort. The flat roof, as large as a football field, was lined with battlements, like a medieval castle, while one corner of the mansion was anchored by a rectangular Italian

Renaissance–style tower and the other by a round, tur-
reted tower that looked like it might be home to Sleeping
Beauty.

The limousine pulled away.

"Come, come," Miss Reynolds insisted, hurrying up
the stairs and opening one of the enormous wooden
front doors, indicating with a sweep of her hand that
they were to enter before her. "I'm afraid it's the servants'
night off, and so I'm unable to greet you as formally as I'd
like. No butler. A mere rented limousine, rather than my
personal chauffeur. Please, I mean no offense."

"No offense taken," Aunt Judith said as she entered
the mansion.

"Your hospitality is exemplary," Uncle Jack assured
his hostess as he reached the doorway and politely indicated that she was to go inside before him.

She nodded and went in.

With tail held high, Roderick followed her.

Uncle Jack turned to his nephews. "Best behavior,
boys," he whispered as he ushered them inside.

"Why not?" they answered.

They had nothing against Miss Reynolds. It was her
ancestor who'd been the murderer.

WHAT THE POE TWINS DID NOT KNOW …
A LETTER DELIVERED THREE DAYS BEFORE TO THE
GREEN SPRING VALLEY MANSION

IGER COFFIN MAKERS
Serving discreet customers since 1845

Dear Professor,

First, allow me to express my sympathies for the law enforcement interference that befell you last year. What a shame that the luxurious child-size coffin we delivered to your Kansas location is now in the hands of the authorities, empty. On a brighter note, it is my pleasure to inform you that we can offer you free overnight shipping of a replacement child-size coffin to your Maryland address. Additionally, because you are a valued customer, we will include our deluxe cat-size coffin at no charge.

As for your invitation to be your personal guest for the big night, I couldn't be more thrilled to accept. I will bring a bottle of Dom Pérignon champagne, vintage 1959, to toast your achievement.

Sincerely,

Markus Iger, Esq.

A DINNER TO DIE FOR

THE foyer of the mansion was roughly the size and height of a racquetball court, decorated from floor to ceiling with dozens of life-size portraits of Victorian ladies and gentlemen. There, Miss Reynolds made the formal acquaintance of Uncle Jack, who shook her hand, and Aunt Judith, who actually started to curtsy.

Roderick sat formally before her.

"Ah, and this is your famous cat," Miss Reynolds observed politely as she bent to pat his head.

"Roderick Usher," the twins said as an introduction.

"Delightful!" she said, rising.

But the twins noticed that she wiped her hands as if, despite her consistent smile, she found something distasteful about having touched their cat.

They wondered about her sincerity.

"And, of course, I've already had the pleasure of meeting your wonderful boys," she said to Uncle Jack and Aunt Judith. "Such outstanding public speakers. To say nothing of their skills as . . . amateur detectives."

"Yes, their interests are diverse," Aunt Judith answered proudly.

"We're grateful that you're willing to settle this old family matter for us," Uncle Jack said.

"I'd call answering for the murder of America's greatest writer more than a mere family matter," Miss Reynolds replied. "And I mean that both for you Poes and for me."

"Well, honesty is the best policy,"

Aunt Judith said, reverting to the comfort of one of her many favorite sayings.

"Please join me in the parlor," Miss Reynolds said, leading them out of the foyer. "We'll get to the more serious matter of justice shortly. But first, you are my dinner guests, and I have delightful surprises for all of you."

The parlor was sumptuously decorated, but it was not the tasteful art on the walls or the antique curios in the chiffonier or the eighteenth-century Persian rugs or the early-twentieth-century Tiffany lamps that grabbed the Poe family's attention. Rather, it was the delicious and aromatic spread of appetizers arranged elegantly on a long, antique Oriental table set against one wall.

"Mmmm," Uncle Jack murmured. "Beignets."

The New Orleans pastry had become his favorite food during the recent movie shoot in the French Quarter. Judging from the aroma, these were just out of the deep fryer.

"And Camembert cheese with water crackers," Aunt Judith marveled, turning wide-eyed to Miss Reynolds. "How'd you know that was my favorite?"

Miss Reynolds merely smiled.

For Edgar and Allan, there were dark chocolate truffles, the twins' favorite.

"Nothing sets a welcoming tone better than good, personally chosen hors d'oeuvres," Miss Reynolds said, beaming. With a wave of her hand, she motioned the family toward the opulent spread. "Please."

Uncle Jack was first to oblige. "With beignets and chocolate as appetizers, I can hardly imagine what's for dessert," he commented, confectioners' sugar showering down on his suit jacket as he took his first bite.

"I believe in sometimes mixing courses in unconventional ways," Miss Reynolds said. "Oh, I'm happy to serve ordinary appetizers for most people, but if your preference happens to be for sweets, then why *not* start with them?" She stood near Uncle Jack and lowered her voice as if sharing a confidence. "Some of my society friends call me uncouth, but none of them ever leaves my home without a full belly and a smile."

Uncle Jack swallowed a bite. "Uncouth? I call you commonsensical."

"Yes, Miss Reynolds," Aunt Judith agreed. "You're most generous." She picked up a small sterling silver knife, spread a layer of Camembert cheese onto a water cracker, and took a ladylike bite.

"Boys?" Miss Reynolds asked, turning to them.

They shook their heads no.

"What's wrong?" she inquired.

"It's thoughtful of you to have all this here for us," Edgar said.

"But what about Roderick?" Allan asked.

Roderick sat at the twins' feet. He bore an expression of injured neglect.

Miss Reynolds smiled and turned back to the laden table. She removed a sterling silver cover from a small serving plate, revealing rows of glistening pink flesh sliced almost as thin as paper.

"Sashimi-grade tuna," she said, addressing Roderick.

Roderick's expression of neglect turned to one of delight.

Miss Reynolds put the serving plate on the floor.

Roderick sprang forward.

Edgar and Allan joined in at the table, delighting in truffle after chocolate truffle. Delicious! The rich truffles were so good that they even wrapped a few in a napkin and snuck them into their pockets for later.

Miss Reynolds poured imported water into crystal glasses for the Poes and set one on the floor for Roderick.

"And what about you, Miss Reynolds?" Aunt Judith asked, spreading more Camembert on another cracker. "Aren't you joining us in your wonderful banquet?"

Miss Reynolds shook her head regretfully. "I've a health condition that severely limits my diet."

"Oh!" Aunt Judith exclaimed. "I'm so sorry."

"Don't be," Miss Reynolds replied. "I enjoy watching all of you enjoy."

"How'd you know what we all liked?" Uncle Jack asked. The twins had wondered that too.

"Oh, your family is quite famous since the adventures in Kansas and New Orleans," she said. "I read about you in the newspaper and on the Internet. The articles were full of those personal details."

"Ah, I see," Uncle Jack said, satisfied by her answer— and by his second beignet.

But Edgar and Allan looked at each other, suspicious.

Their shared thoughts raced through the possibilities. Yes, they'd mentioned in a newspaper article that they liked dark chocolate truffles and that Roderick's favorite dish was tuna sashimi. And, yes, Uncle Jack had waxed eloquent to *New Orleans Dining Monthly* about his love of beignets. But had Aunt Judith ever mentioned how fond she was of Camembert cheese with water crackers anywhere?

They looked at Miss Reynolds cautiously.

Had they been careless?

This reminded them of the mysterious greeting cards they'd discovered in the limousine and from which they'd been distracted almost immediately.

It was no time to stay distracted.

"You boys suddenly look so serious," Miss Reynolds commented, her voice oozing hospitality. "Isn't the food to your liking? The truffles come from a famous chocolatier in Turin, Italy."

Turin! the boys thought, their memory jogged.

That was the city pictured on the identical greeting cards. And if the town was Turin, then that would make the river pictured flowing through it the Po.

Spelled differently, yes.

But, still, *P-O* as in *P-O-E*.

Next, the boys recalled what had been written inside, the quote from their great-great-great-great granduncle's story "William Wilson":

> Thus it appeared, I say, but was not. It was my antagonist . . . not a line in all the marked and singular lineaments of his face which was not, even in the most absolute identity, *mine own*!

In a flash, the twins realized what the greeting cards were warning them—that the figure in the library, whom they'd taken for the ghost of Edgar Allan Poe, was an identical double. And, worse, that he was *their* antagonist, Professor Perry, who'd slipped back into the country in disguise.

"Gee, I'm not feeling so well," murmured Uncle Jack.

"Maybe you shouldn't *start* a meal with sugary dough-nuts," Aunt Judith whispered to him.

"They're beignets, not doughnuts," he whispered back.

She began to answer, but then her expression changed. "Actually, I'm feeling a little light-headed myself."

The boys paid scant attention to their aunt and uncle,

continuing to analyze their sudden new understanding:

If the ghost in the library was a fraud, then the clue, "Reynolds," must likewise be false, meaning that the Poes' presence in this mansion had nothing to do with solving any 165-year-old murder. Their great-great-great-great granduncle probably hadn't even been murdered! And so this woman had no ancient family secret to confess. They doubted her name was even Reynolds.

The twins looked at each other, identically disconcerted.

And mortified.

She had lured them here in the only way that was possible—by letting Edgar and Allan think that *they* were the ones being clever.

"We have to get out of here, Uncle Jack and Aunt Judith," Allan told them. "Now!"

"It's a trap!" added Edgar.

But their uncle and aunt looked at them with seeming incomprehension, their expressions hazy.

Miss Reynolds, or whoever she really was, turned to the twins. "Enjoy your chocolates, boys?" she asked, not bothering to conceal a new, devious joy. "They really are imported. Just like the tasteless, odorless Mickey that the professor and I injected into all your family's lovely appetizers."

Roderick Usher dropped unconscious on the luxurious Persian rug.

Uncle Jack and Aunt Judith stumbled toward the couch, falling like rag dolls across its stiff brocade, out cold.

"Do you know what a Mickey is, boys?" she asked.

"It's slang for a knockout drug," Allan managed to answer.

"Excellent," she said sarcastically. "Vocab champs right to the very end."

Edgar and Allan started toward her.

But they didn't get far.

The last thing they glimpsed as they collapsed to the floor was their great-great-great-great granduncle entering the room; the last thing they thought before losing consciousness was that, of course, it was not the ghost of Edgar Allan Poe, but their nemesis, Professor S. Pangborn Perry in disguise.

And then all went black.

WHAT THE POE TWINS DID NOT KNOW . . .
GUEST LIST FOR PROFESSOR PERRY'S
CELEBRATORY DINNER PARTY

From the Desk of
PROFESSOR S. PANGBORN PERRY, PhD

1. Me

2. Barbara Bainbridge, actress (aka Miss Birdy Reynolds)

3. Markus Iger, coffin maker

4. Dr. Psufo, cosmetic surgeon (from Shanghai)

5. Ian Archer, personal assistant (recently freed from Leavenworth prison, Kansas—by me, of course!)

CAPTIVE AUDIENCE

WHEN a groggy Edgar and Allan simultaneously opened their eyes, they found themselves in a filthy basement illuminated only by the moonlight that streamed through a small window fifteen feet overhead. Worse, they were tied beside one another, faceup, on narrow tables. Worse yet, a few feet above them was a glittering, sharp, foot-long curved blade at the bottom of a long pole that reached up into the shadows. They tried to pull themselves free, but the ropes held them tight.

This was not a good way to wake up.

"Feeling a little headachy?" asked a husky, unfamiliar female voice.

Edgar and Allan turned their heads, which indeed ached from the knockout drug. It was Miss Reynolds, standing in the open doorway at the foot of the stairs that led up to the house.

"Yes, this is my real voice, boys," she said, kicking up dust as she moved into the basement. "I have many voices and dialects, as I am a professional actress known off-Broadway and in regional theaters as Barbara Bainbridge."

She waited a moment, as if the name might mean something to the twins.

It didn't.

"My performance in Neil Simon's *The Goodbye Girl* at the Princess Theater in Spokane, Washington, is still legendary," she said huffily. "Of course, of late I've enjoyed bringing a little blue-blooded vulnerability to my most recent role as Birdy Reynolds."

The boys tried to speak, but their heads were still too cloudy.

"Actually, I'm from Duluth, Minnesota," she continued. "I'm no millionaire's daughter. But Professor Perry is a marvelous director. He helped me to make my character truly convincing. I fooled you two, right?"

"Was Mrs. Rosecrans in on this?" Allan managed.

"No, I fooled her too."

"Why would you do this?" Edgar asked, straining to get the words out.

"Because the professor paid me a *lot* of money," she

answered. "Besides, I'm always up for a professional challenge. Acting is, after all, my life. And truthfully, I don't like children very much."

"Fine, you fooled us," Edgar murmured. Once again he strained uselessly at the ropes that held him to the table. "You're an excellent actress. So, now you can untie us."

She shook her head. "My part in this drama may be over, my place relegated now to the wings—but yours is just beginning, boys." She placed one of her manicured hands gently on Allan's shoe. Then she looked up. "Since you two are such precocious readers, and Poes to boot, I'm sure I don't have to explain the purpose of that glittering scythe suspended above you."

Naturally, the twins had read "The Pit and the Pendulum."

They knew a deadly torture device when they saw one.

"Where are our aunt and uncle?" Edgar mumbled, shaking his head hard to clear it.

"And Roderick?" Allan added, managing to move his foot just enough to dislodge her hand.

"What admirable characters you are," she said melodramatically. "Concerned about the welfare of others, even as a truly horrible fate hangs just a few feet above you."

From upstairs, someplace far off in the mansion, a melodious handbell rang.

"Ah, that'll be the appetizers being served," she said. Then she winked. "The *real* appetizers. No Mickeys."

The bell rang again, this time more emphatically.

She held her finger to her lips. "He doesn't know I'm down here," she stage-whispered. "But I couldn't resist coming. After all, I *do* so enjoy meeting my public. Nonetheless, I must go back upstairs. You see, we're sharing a celebratory dinner with the professor's colleagues and admirers. Oh, there'll be delicacies from all over the world." She looked from one tied-down boy to the other. "Adieu, adieu—parting is such sweet sorrow, boys."

Then she moved across the basement, closed a heavy door after herself, and went up the stairs.

In the silence, the twins now heard only the scampering and squeaking of rats.

"We have to do something," Allan murmured.

"Right," Edgar agreed.

But with their heads still polluted by the knockout drug, the twins couldn't do much.

☞☠☜

Thirty minutes later, the door to the basement opened again. Edgar and Allan felt much clearer of mind, though they remained tightly lashed to their respective tabletops. All that their twisting and tugging had accomplished was to deepen the rope burns at their wrists. Now, turning their heads toward the sound, they saw in the light of the open door the image of Edgar Allan Poe. It was a strange and disconcerting sight. But they no longer had any doubts as to this man's true identity.

"Professor Perry," Edgar said, spitting out the words as if they held a bad taste.

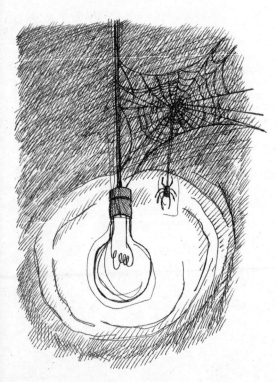

"Hello, brats," the professor answered, closing the door behind him. Stopping beside his captives, he reached up and pulled a string that hung parallel to the arm of the deadly pendulum. A single exposed lightbulb illuminated the ill-tended basement—spiders and rats scurried for the shadows. "Comfortable?" the professor asked.

"I'm afraid you're in for a disappointment," Edgar said boldly.

The professor chuckled. "Oh?"

The twins had failed to loosen their bonds, but they had not wasted their time in this dank place. Returning to their senses, they'd come to a startling realization.

"Your plan to kill one of us and keep the other as a communications channel to the next world won't work, Professor Perry," Allan said almost gleefully.

"So you may as well let us go, along with Roderick and our aunt and uncle, and then we *might* be willing to call it even," Edgar added, lifting his head to get a look at the professor's expression. "Assuming you vow never to bother us again."

The professor's chuckle turned to a full guffaw.

The twins were not discouraged.

"As you know, Professor, my brother and I learned in New Orleans how it works with the dead," Edgar continued. "Your spy, Miss Reynolds—or Miss Bainbridge, or whoever she is—heard our speech about Monsieur and Madame Du Valier. All about how it works with murder victims. She must have reported back, and you, being of passable intelligence, planned the ruse that brought us here in pursuit of our own great-great-great-great grand-uncle's murderer, even though he'd never *been* murdered."

"Yes, a beautiful trap, isn't it?" he asked, crossing his arms and leaning back with utmost satisfaction. It was truly disgusting to see that expression on their ancestor's face. "Particularly as I'd already chosen Poe's likeness for the reconstructive facial surgery I'd had done in Shanghai to fool the authorities when I reentered the USA."

"Admittedly clever," Allan acknowledged. "And fortuitous for you. But don't you see? If you murder one of us, then he'll be trapped in this world as a ghost, *unable* to move on until his murder has been solved or avenged. We didn't know that in Kansas, when you first explained your deviant plan. But now we do. Thus, even if you keep one of us prisoner, you'll have no contact with the next world because the murder victim will be trapped here. Do you understand, Professor?"

He shook his head. "Oh, it'll work, so long as I write a full confession, signed Professor S. Pangborn Perry."

"Yes, but then you'll go to prison."

The professor motioned to his face. "How will the authorities recognize me, geniuses?"

"But—" the boys started.

Perry held up one finger, as if anticipating their objection. "Recall, boys, that back in New Orleans you two didn't *punish* the murderous pirate. He was already long dead. You just brought his *name* to public disgrace, which proved enough to set your ghostly friends free. Thus, my signed confession will set the murdered one of you free. And then I'll simply adopt a new name to go with my new face."

Could he be right?

Gleefully, Professor Perry slapped his hand down on one of the tables. "Ha!" he laughed. "If you really want to talk about unsolved homicides whose victims are trapped where they were killed, well, we could talk about your mother and father, who are orbiting the Earth even as we speak, soon to crash at some random spot in a final, obliterating fireball."

"They died in an accident," Allan said.

"Oh, *did they*?" Professor Perry asked pointedly. He grinned. "Mal and Irma Poe didn't like my private scientific observations of their remarkable twin boys. Of course, I never told them my *full* plan. But, still, they took a dislike to me and demanded I stay away. So I drugged them, just as I drugged you, right before they went up for final adjustments to the satellite. And three, two, one, whoosh! Gone."

"You murdered them!" the boys shouted, straining uselessly at the ropes.

"That's such a *harsh* word," Professor Perry answered. "I prefer the word 'eliminated.' But if 'murder' is what you want to call it, who am I to object?"

The harmonious handbell rang upstairs.

"Ah, that means the main course is being served," Professor Perry said. "So, I'm afraid I have to leave you boys for a little while. But perhaps I'll bring back dessert—for one of you, at least."

He pointed a small remote control toward the top of the deadly pendulum, which responded by beginning to swing in gradually widening arcs. The boys watched the glimmering blade swooping back and forth above them.

"You know how it works from my . . ." The professor laughed. "I mean, your ancestor's story. The blade will gradually descend, giving you time to consider your terrible fate. The only difference is that, at the last moment, the arm of this device will slip randomly into one of two brackets so as to slice only one of you in half. After all, it wouldn't do for me to come back from dinner to find the two of you in four parts. I only want three."

"What have you done with our aunt and uncle?" Allan demanded, unable to take his eyes from the swinging blade.

"And Roderick!" Edgar added.

"Your aunt and uncle are a little *tied up* right now," he answered with a laugh. "I'll deal with them later. But your cat . . . Well, that creature has caused me much trouble in the past. I couldn't allow that to happen again. So he's gone."

"Gone?" the twins asked, full of trepidation.

The professor laughed again. "Your cat's tuna sashimi was not spiked with a knockout drug like the other appetizers, but was infused with *deadly* toxin from the fugu fish. Does that make me a murderer? Or just bad around cats?"

"You're lying!" the boys cried.

"No." The professor smirked. "I'm not."

The boys believed him, though they didn't want to. Stunned, they couldn't speak.

"Poison seemed the best choice," the professor continued. "Oh, sure, there are bloodier, more satisfying ways of taking revenge on an enemy, be it a human or feline. But I can't stand the sound of caterwauling *or* screaming. Call me a softie. Which explains why I've arranged for your imminent, bloody encounter with the razor-sharp pendulum to occur while I'm upstairs, dining peaceably. I mean, who likes the sound of a child's screams? After all, I'm not some kind of maniac. Well, then again . . ." He grinned as he removed from his pocket a large, old-fashioned key.

The twins still had only one terrible thought: *Roderick dead . . .*

Professor Perry exited, closing and locking the heavy wooden door behind him.

The foot-long blade at the end of the pendulum kept swooshing back and forth, gradually descending.

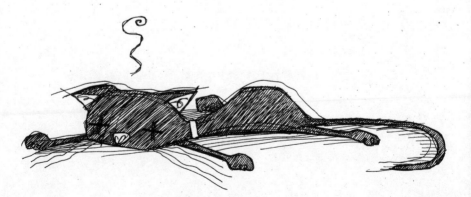

WHAT THE POE TWINS DID NOT KNOW . . .

Menu for Professor Perry's
Celebratory Dinner Party
International Flavors!

Appetizers

WASP CRACKERS: Japanese wasps, boiled, dried, and infused into wafers

CASU MARZU: A Sardinian sheep milk cheese, uniquely flavored by live insect larvae

NATTO: Fermented soybean jelly

FRIED TARANTULA: Imported live from Cambodia, prepared here

Soup

STINK HEADS SOUP: Rotting Alaskan salmon heads in a savory broth

Entrées

SMALAHOVE: Norwegian smoked sheep's head

HÁKARL: An Icelandic preparation of fermented basking shark

BLOOD SAUSAGE

STEAMED BROCCOLI AND CARROTS

Desserts

DURIAN: This fragrant fruit is banned in many public places for its distinctive scent

SUN-DRIED TOMATO SORBET WITH BALSAMIC VINEGAR

Beverages

MEKONG RIVER EEL WINE

COFFEE OR TEA

RATS!

EDGAR and Allan could barely muster the energy to attempt an escape. Not with Roderick gone. They missed him already. Who wouldn't? He was the smartest cat in the world, though they'd have loved him even if he had been average in every way. And they blamed themselves. How could they have led poor Roderick into the professor's trap? Tears streamed down the sides of their faces until they hadn't any tears left.

Uncle Jack and Aunt Judith were captive upstairs, awaiting the professor's mortal wrath. . . .

And now the twins knew that their parents, too, had been murdered. Mal and Irma Poe had been ghosts all these years, trapped in their orbiting satellite tomb, which was soon to crash, possibly killing many more.

Lesser boys might not have been able to carry on. But

Edgar and Allan were not going to be part of the professor's plan, no matter how much he had schemed. Their beloved aunt and uncle were not going to die. And, most of all, Professor Perry was not going to be allowed to get away with any of it—especially since bringing him to justice would set Mal and Irma Poe free to move on from this world, and so too Roderick, *if* the ghost business worked the same with animals.

Rage inspired the twins now.

Still, the razor-sharp pendulum swung above them. And it had already lowered a foot and a half. Any minute, it would begin to slice one of the boys into two bloody pieces.

Untying the ropes would have been easy for Roderick.

Edgar and Allan had to come up with something.

"OK," Allan said, taking a deep, sobering breath as the blade swung overhead. "Let's think about the actual story that our great-great-great-great granduncle wrote."

In "The Pit and the Pendulum," the main character escapes the descending blade that swings over *his* heart by rubbing oily food on the ropes that bind him, thereby drawing the rats who share the dark pit. It is no picnic to have ravenous rodents crawl all over his body, but the animals' enthusiastic gnawing ultimately sets him free.

"There are rats here," Edgar observed.

"And we have chocolates," Allan said. "Albeit drugged chocolates."

The boys could move their hands just enough to reach into their pockets for the truffles they'd taken earlier.

"Let's hope there are enough sweet-toothed rats in here to get the job done before the last of them passes out," Edgar said.

Twisting and straining their wrists, the twins rubbed the half-melted chocolates on the ropes. Soon, the rats began to creep out of the basement shadows, cautiously interested. Edgar and Allan lay still, not wanting to spook them. Unfortunately, the swinging pendulum kept the rodents at bay for a while.

"We don't have much time!" Allan whispered.

At last, one brave rat scurried up a table leg. He scampered over Edgar's chest, his tiny, clawed feet like so many pinpricks. Edgar struggled to remain still. It wasn't easy to let a rat scrabble over him. And it only got harder when the other rats, encouraged by their leader's success, joined the party. Soon, both boys were literally crawling with rats.

"Ugh!" Edgar whispered.

Then more rats.

Finally, both boys had to bite down on their tongues to keep from screaming.

Meantime, the rats kept gnawing on the chocolate-flavored sections of the ropes—as well as the twins' chocolaty pockets, which was even worse. Nonetheless, it seemed to be working!

Sections of the ropes were beginning to fray.

Then one of the rats passed out cold.

Then another rat and another fell off the boys' chests and onto the ground. The latecomers kept gnawing, even as their compatriots kept passing out beside them. But how long could these last rats keep at it, however delicious the chocolate-flavored ropes?

Rats are much smaller than boys, so the knockout drug acted fast.

And the pendulum was so close now that the twins could feel the breeze each time it passed.

The last pair of rats slid off the boys' chests, unconscious.

The ropes still held.

Edgar moved his right wrist. "There are only a few strands left!" he said to Allan. Both boys worked their hands and arms, their sweating faces fanned by the swinging scythe.

And then—*snap!*—the chewed ropes fell off the table.

The twins contorted themselves to unknot the rest of the ropes as the pendulum descended ever lower. They ducked and dodged the blade.

Finally, all the knots were undone—and Edgar and Allan were free!

They rolled off the wooden tables, careful not to step on any of the dazed rodents who had freed them. Seconds later, the pendulum slipped into a bracket and the curved blade descended with sudden, terrible violence on the left table, slicing a straight, shallow line in the wood exactly where one of the boys had lain just seconds before.

Edgar and Allan looked at each other.

They were glad to be alive. But Roderick . . .

They hadn't time to mourn. That would come later.

There were still too many immediate problems to solve.

For example: how to get out of this locked basement?

The window was fifteen feet above them—too high
to reach, even if they made a pile of scattered junk

and climbed up. Besides, there were steel bars on the window.

Still, there had to be a way out.

Skirting the battalion of still-unconscious rats, Edgar and Allan tried knocking on all the walls, looking for a hollow spot. If they found one, they could take the deadly pendulum apart and use the blade to slice through the drywall into whatever other underground room might lie adjacent—ideally, a chamber that offered some means of escape.

Not a bad plan.

However, all that their knocking revealed was that the basement was as solid as if it had been carved out of rock.

The twins looked at each other. There was too much at stake to fail.

But how to get out?

Edgar and Allan reasoned: Since the rats had gotten into the basement, then it couldn't be truly sealed. And by the dim moonlight that illuminated the room, the twins indeed found a few openings near the base of the walls. However, these allowed for nothing larger than a rat.

"We can figure out a way to take down the pendulum

and use it as a weapon for when the professor comes back," Allan suggested.

"A kind of spear?" Edgar added hopefully. "Or long battle-ax!"

Allan nodded.

But after a moment, both boys realized it was a doomed plan. Professor Perry likely carried a pistol, which he'd use the moment he saw the dismantled pendulum turned on him.

Edgar brightened. "OK, so what if we remove the blade and rig a trap so it drops on the professor just as he opens the door, slicing him in half as he hoped to slice one of us?"

"That's good, but how do we rig it?" Allan asked.

The ceiling was too high to reach.

"Then how about if one of us throws the blade at him? I mean, look at it. It's shaped like a boomerang, which for millennia has been an effective hunting tool for Australian Aborigines."

"Yeah, but if we miss? With a razor-sharp *boomerang*?"

"Oh, right."

Since the boys had just avoided getting themselves sliced in half, this was not a good idea.

So, what now?

WHAT THE POE TWINS DID NOT KNOW . . .
ON THE PROFESSOR'S MP3 PLAYER

‹ PLAYLISTS

TONIGHT'S AFTER-DINNER MUSIC:
MY FAVORITE MOMENTS IN OPERA

The death of Butterfly
Madama Butterfly, **Puccini** ›

The death of Mimì
La Bohème, **Puccini** ›

The death of Tosca
Tosca, **Puccini** ›

The death of Rodrigo
Don Carlo, **Verdi** ›

"When I Am Laid in Earth"
Dido and Aeneas, **Purcell** ›

The mad scene
Lucia di Lammermoor, **Donizetti** ›

Mr. Poe in the Great Beyond

Mr. Poe stood alone in the tiny break room of the Animal Languages Division. In one hand, he held a porcelain cup containing coffee that had long before cooled to room temperature. In the other hand, he held a copy of the brilliant greeting card that Emily Dickinson had managed to smuggle down to the Poe twins—just moments too late to save them. Mr. Poe's expression was sad and faraway.

He'd left his desk and come here immediately after Edgar and Allan lost consciousness at the hors d'oeuvres table in the mansion down on Earth. He couldn't watch the horrors he suspected were bound to follow.

During his lifetime, Mr. Poe had written about many grisly deaths. But that didn't mean he ever got used to them happening in real life.

Especially to those he loved.

An announcement over the office PA system snapped him out of his dark reverie. "Mr. Poe to the reception area. Mr. Poe to reception."

He sighed.

The last thing he wanted to do was to show another newly arrived animal—an ostrich or gnu or sloth or boa constrictor—around the place, pointing out the supplies closet and the water cooler and the copy machine, and finally concluding the tour at the animal's new cubicle. But since Mr. Poe had recently refused to waste any more time attempting to make coherent speech out of animal grunts and groans, this task of showing newcomers around had become his responsibility—Mr. Shakespeare's idea, of course.

He poured the cold coffee down the drain without ever having taken a sip of it, sighed, and started for the reception area.

There, he was met by a surprise that both overjoyed him and broke his heart.

It was no ordinary new arrival.

"My old friend!" he said to the black cat with the figure-eight marking on his chest.

The cat leaped into Mr. Poe's arms.

It was good to hold his one-time pet, who purred affectionately. Mr. Poe rested his cheek softly against the top of the cat's head. This was just what he needed to pull him from his despair. But he also knew how painful it had to be for his nephews, who had lost their friend— and to make matters worse, might not know that all animals go straight to the next world, regardless of the way they die.

He sighed again as Roderick purred.

Then he held the cat at arm's length to get a better look at him.

For a dead cat, he was in great shape.

In Mr. Poe's lifetime, the two had been more than just master and pet. They'd been great friends. In those days, the cat had been a tortoiseshell and bore a black number six where he now bore a white figure eight. The years spent in Baltimore with Mr. Poe had constituted the sixth of nine lives.

Roderick's seventh life had been spent among artists and writers on the Left Bank of Paris in the 1920s. That time, he'd been a gray tabby and bore a number seven.

His eighth he'd spent happily with Edgar and Allan. Now he had only one life left.

The vast majority of old wives' tales are pure fabrication, but the one about cats having nine lives is actually true. Most cats space out those nine lives, sometimes waiting centuries before returning to be reborn on Earth.

But Roderick wasn't most cats.

Mr. Poe carried him into the restroom for privacy, locking the door behind them. He didn't want their reunion interrupted by inquisitive elephants or nosy crocodiles. "The twins?" he asked.

"Meow," Roderick answered.

"Still alive!" Mr. Poe cried in delight and surprise.

Just as surprising was that Mr. Poe understood the *meow* as if it had been English. It didn't work that way with any of the other animals here. And it went far beyond the way many pet lovers understand their pets on Earth. Perhaps it was a combination of familiarity and being in the Animal Languages Division? No matter. Mr. Poe wasn't going to waste time trying to figure it out—not with the twins' lives in the balance.

"Meow, meow!" Roderick continued.

Mr. Poe's expression changed to one of concern. "That's very brave, but reckless. After all, my friend, if you use your ninth life right now to go back in the guise of your former self, well . . . you'll lose all the kitten years of your final life, thereby shortening it. And, even worse, you'll be delivering yourself into grave danger when you can least afford to do so."

"Meow," Roderick said.

"Yes, I agree it's important. But what, exactly, can you do to help the twins?"

Roderick had no specific answer for this one. But it seemed logical to them both that his return, being wholly unexpected to Professor Perry, was bound to have some kind of positive effect.

That's when the pounding on the bathroom door started. And the angry roar. A grizzly bear needed the toilet.

Always a bad idea to make grizzlies wait.

"Let's go to my cubicle," Mr. Poe suggested.

The grizzly stepped aside as they exited, but flashed Mr. Poe an impatient look.

"Don't worry, I put the seat down," Mr. Poe assured the bear.

Once at Mr. Poe's cubicle, the two old friends picked up their conversation.

"Meow," Roderick said.

"Yes, I know they've taught you new skills," Mr. Poe acknowledged. "The rope stuff and the playing dead and all the vocal impressions—dogs, birds, crying babies. Excellent. But how can we put any of those things to use?"

The cat purred. Then he said, "Meow."

Mr. Poe nodded. "I understand. You're determined to go back. I guess I'd do the same if I could. Still, my friend, this means we have to say good-bye again."

Roderick softly chirruped.

"You're right. I'll see you again, in time," Mr. Poe acknowledged.

A familiar voice called from across the office. "Mr. Poe?" It was Emily Dickinson, who didn't seem to mind the gamy smell of the animals and the generally disorderly atmosphere.

Mr. Poe spun his desk chair around.

No one wore a high-collared black cotton dress more attractively, he thought.

She stopped at the entrance to his cubicle. "Our greeting card warning?" she inquired. "Did it work?"

Mr. Poe shook his head. "It was too late, I'm afraid."

Her face fell. "Oh, I'm so sorry."

"It's not your fault, Emily. The card was brilliant."

Miss Dickinson wrung her hands. "But the boys, what shall—"

"Don't worry. Roderick's got a plan."

She turned to the black cat with the figure eight on his chest. "Roderick? Roderick Usher?" She realized what this meant. She sighed. "So, the professor managed to . . ." She couldn't finish the sentence.

"Meow," answered Roderick.

Miss Dickinson didn't understand.

"It was poison," Mr. Poe translated.

"I'm so sorry," she said. Then she clenched her fists. "We have to help the boys. Somehow!"

"We will," Mr. Poe assured her. "You see, my friend here is the bravest feline in this world or any other."

NEVERMORE

"A tunnel?" Edgar proposed, glancing down, desperate to find any way out of the basement.

The floor *was* dirt.

Allan stomped his foot. "But it's hard as rock."

That's when they heard a most unexpected sound just outside the heavy, locked wooden door that led to the steps upstairs.

A baby crying softly.

Edgar and Allan made their way to the heavy door, pressing their ears against it.

The sound of the baby's cries turned to the chirping of a sparrow.

The twins looked at each other, confused.

Then the chirping was replaced by the sound of a monkey chattering.

Baby cries, sparrows, monkeys? These were vocal impersonations the twins had taught to—

There was a familiar meow.

The boys held their breaths. Was it the murdered Roderick's ghost?

They glanced cautiously at the doorknob. They'd heard the professor turn the old-fashioned key to lock it.

Nonetheless, Allan tried the knob.

To their surprise, the door opened.

Sitting on one of the lower steps that led out of the basement was Roderick, the key in his mouth.

The twins were overjoyed. But confused. "Are you a ghost?" Edgar asked Roderick.

As if in answer, the cat leaped into his arms.

Ghosts may look like ordinary beings, but they don't
feel like warm flesh and blood.

"But we thought . . ." Allan started. He stopped. What
was the use of telling Roderick about the terrible scare
they'd had a few minutes before, the deep sense that
they'd truly lost him forever?

Roderick purred. It was a beautiful sound.

Then, in the dim light, Edgar noticed something
strange. He held Roderick away from him, observing the
cat's chest—there, in place of the familiar white figure
eight, was a patch of white fur in the shape of a nine.

"Roderick," Edgar asked, "is this really you?"

Roderick gave him a disgruntled look, as if to say,
How dare you ask?

"But the nine?" Allan inquired.

Roderick meowed. However, what translated into
English up in the Animal Languages Division did not do
the same on Earth.

So the twins looked at each other, uncertain.

There was one way to confirm this was really their
cat.

Allan said, "Lo! in yon brilliant window-niche, how
statue-like I see thee stand." This quote, from one of their

great-great-great-great granduncle's works, served as one of two cues for the Stuffed Cat Trick, known only to Roderick and the twins.

In response, the black cat froze and his eyes went glassy, as if he were an inanimate work of feline taxidermy.

"It *is* you!" The boys rejoiced.

Roderick snapped back to life.

But the white, furry *nine*?

The twins looked at each other.

Maybe it was just a strange, feline reaction to the apparently nonfatal fugu fish that Roderick had eaten. Or might the numeral stand for something mystical, such as the transition from an eighth life into a ninth life?

Nah, the twins thought. That nine lives business was strictly an old wives' tale.

Wasn't it?

In any case, this was no time for contemplation.

"We've much to do," Edgar said.

"Starting with finding Uncle Jack and Aunt Judith," said his brother.

But Roderick seemed suddenly distracted, glancing around Edgar and into the basement. He began licking his chops and squirming in the boy's arms.

Edgar and Allan turned.

The rats were regaining consciousness, and as they caught sight of Roderick, their tiny, luminous eyes widened. Squeaking, they began to pour out of the house through the rat holes and into the cold night.

Roderick tried to go after them.

Edgar held tight. "Hey, those guys saved our lives," he said to Roderick.

Roderick gave them a confused look.

"Just trust me," Edgar assured him as he started up the stairs after Allan.

At the top of the basement stairs, the boys opened the door very slowly.

All clear.

Edgar set Roderick on the thick carpet, and he and his brother tiptoed into the mansion behind their soft-footed cat. They knew that in the dining room their mortal enemies were now enjoying a meal in celebration of Edgar's or Allan's presumed gruesome death. Over soaring, throbbing operatic music, the twins could make out the sound of talking, though they couldn't make out the words. Nonetheless, the tone was evident—it was jubilant, arrogant, barbarous.

Roderick started toward the grand staircase, which

lay in the direction of the dining room.

The twins followed, trying to step as lightly as their cat.

At the foot of the staircase, they now could make out the words. They stopped to listen:

Miss Reynolds—or, rather, the actress Barbara Bainbridge—spoke in her naturally husky voice. "So, according to the latest update on my phone, NASA has confirmed that the satellite will destroy most of downtown Baltimore!"

The twins looked at each other, horrified. *Baltimore?*

Stevie "The Hulk" Harrison, Katie Justus, David Litke, Riley McHuff . . .

Mrs. Rosecrans and all the teachers!

And thousands of others!

"Ha!" Professor Perry laughed among his company of villains. "Considering that's where those rocket scientists came from—well, isn't it deliciously ironic? What a ripe turn of events!"

The others at the table laughed with him, their dinnerware rattling.

"Should be quite a boon to my business," said a man whose voice the twins didn't recognize.

"So true, Mr. Iger," the professor responded. "With

less than fifteen minutes until impact, Baltimore is pretty much doomed. Look at this video on my phone. Can you see it? Go ahead, pass it around. The streets and expressways are jammed. You're going to run out of caskets, Mr. Iger," he concluded brightly.

"Lucky for you, Professor, that I already brought the deluxe units for the boy and the cat," Mr. Iger answered with a chuckle. "Or you might be paying premium prices!"

"And best of all is that with so many dead in Baltimore, no one will ever miss the Poe brats or their pathetic guardians," said a man with a Chinese accent.

"So true, Dr. Psufo," said the professor. "Who knew that crazy, careening satellite would make my life easier?"

"We're lucky to be out here in the country," Mr. Iger responded.

"Do you think we'll hear the explosion and see the flash from all these miles away?" asked Barbara Bainbridge.

"Oh, yes," the professor assured her. "It'll be massive."

"Hundreds or even thousands dead," said another man, whose voice the twins recognized as that of Mr. Ian Archer. He was the professor's right-hand man and was supposed to be imprisoned in Kansas. Doubtless, his boss had sprung him.

Roderick had heard enough. He started up the stairs.

The boys followed him, thinking it through: The Bradbury Telecommunications Satellite was just four-teen minutes from crashing into Baltimore. It would be a catastrophe of epic proportions. Frustratingly, the twins still hadn't deduced the code needed to redirect the craft's guidance system. Since there were a billion possibilities to *any* nine-digit code, even NASA had given up. Still, there had to be *something* the twins could do!

Meantime, Roderick had run to the end of the upstairs hallway, and was now sitting like an Egyptian sculpture before a closed door.

Edgar and Allan hurried toward him.

Along the way, they glanced through the open door-way of one of the other rooms. It appeared to be Professor Perry's office, visible in the moonlight that streamed through a window near the desk. The only other light in the room was the glow of a computer screen.

The boys hesitated a moment, their shared minds racing.

Very softly, Roderick meowed to regain their attention.

The boys nodded and joined their cat at the far door. Inside, they found Uncle Jack and Aunt Judith bound and gagged. Though the pair could not move, their eyes expressed their relieved delight at the sight of Edgar and Allan. Edgar held a finger to his lips. Then Allan began very softly whistling "Ring Around the Rosy," which was Roderick's cue to begin untying the knotted ropes.

The cat leaped to the tied-up couple and began to work.

The twins raced back down the hall to Professor Perry's office computer.

On the table beside the computer, they discovered a handwritten draft of a threatening letter to another scientist. There was no time to read it now, of course, but Allan folded the note and put it in his back pocket.

With the city of Baltimore at stake, the twins knew their aunt and uncle would certainly have no objections to their going online. They bent over the computer, their four hands typing at once, as coordinated as moving parts in a lightning-fast clock.

Hacking into the NASA site was a snap for Edgar and Allan.

And getting into the site for the Bradbury satellite was no more difficult.

But there they stopped.

ACCESS TO GUIDANCE SYSTEM
PASSWORD (NUMBERS ONLY):

_ _ _ _ _ _ _ _

The Poe twins looked at each other, stumped.

Less than twelve minutes before the destruction of their hometown.

And, almost equally frightening, they heard Professor Perry's voice from downstairs. "And now it's on to the dessert course—delicious sliced durian—one serving of which we will set aside to take down to the basement to share with the surviving Poe twin, our captive." Then more laughter.

That's when they heard a *tap-tap-tapping* at the window.

They turned just in time to catch a fluttering shadow outside—two stories up. And then nothing.

"What was that?" Edgar muttered.

Silence. They returned to the computer.

Tap-tap-tap. Tap-tap-tap.

This time, the boys turned and saw a large black bird on the windowsill outside.

A raven.

Allan heaved open the double-paned window and the raven flew inside without hesitation, fluttering about with a black gusto of wings until it came to rest atop the professor's bookshelf, on the head of a sculpted bust of a Greek goddess.

Naturally, the twins thought of their great-great-great-great granduncle's most famous poem, "The Raven." And when the bird pronounced a word with all the clarity of a trained stage actor, the twins knew that this was no coincidence.

The raven said, "Nevermore."

Just like in the poem.

"But what does that have to do with us?" Allan asked, looking at the bird.

"Nevermore," responded the raven.

"Where have you come from?" Edgar asked. "Who sent you?"

"Nevermore."

Does it matter where the bird comes from? the twins wondered.

Or who sent him?

And might there be sense to the word, after all?

"Nevermore!" the twins cried in unison.

The word contained nine letters. . . .

Mal and Irma were rocket scientists, but they were also Poes!

The boys turned back to the computer.

"On a telephone keypad, the word 'nevermore' would be typed as 638376673," Edgar said.

They glanced at the clock at the bottom of the computer screen.

The satellite was due to demolish Baltimore in less than seven minutes.

"Type it in," Allan said.

Edgar did so.

They held their breaths.

After a moment, a new screen appeared:

ACCESS GRANTED

The raven pushed off of the sculpted bust and disappeared out the open window.

The bust teetered and fell to the floor, breaking into thirds.

"If we employ the guidance system, we can still alter

the satellite's point of impact, saving Baltimore," said Allan.

"But we can't reverse its direction to send it into the Atlantic," Edgar observed. "Its angle of momentum is already established."

"So we have to pick a spot in the general Baltimore-DC area."

"Right, but we can't just pick any spot," Edgar added. "We wouldn't know what we'd be destroying."

The boys looked at each other. *This is the spot*, they thought simultaneously.

The mansion.

By entering its geographical coordinates, they could at once save their city and, by directing the satellite's crash, allow for their mother and father's murderers to be avenged, setting Mal and Irma free to move on to wherever it was they truly belonged.

A simple mapping program identified the exact coordinates of the mansion.

The twins typed it into the satellite's guidance system.

CONFIRMED:

COORDINATES CHANGED

A clock on the screen began counting down the time to impact: five minutes, twenty seconds.

"Now we've got to get out of here," Edgar said.

"Roderick ought to be finished untying Uncle Jack and Aunt Judith," Allan added.

They turned.

But the doorway was occupied by a familiar and unwelcome presence—the image of Edgar Allan Poe.

"My, aren't you two slippery?" Professor Perry said. He had a gun trained on them. "I thought I heard something peculiar up here." He stepped over the broken sculpture. "So I took it upon myself to check."

The twins said nothing.

The professor took another step toward them. "I think you boys owe me an apology for making me rudely leave all my guests downstairs, to say nothing of my having to abandon the delicious dessert I was just beginning to enjoy."

The twins stayed silent.

"Hey, what's that countdown on the computer screen?" the professor asked.

WHAT THE POE TWINS DID NOT KNOW...
A NOTE LEFT THAT NIGHT IN THE MAILBOX
OF THE POE HOUSE IN BALTIMORE

Dear Edgar and Allan,

We were in the neighborhood with our parents and thought we'd take a chance and stop by to see if you and your aunt and uncle were home. Sorry to have missed you. Hope you're all having fun, wherever you are. In any case, we're back from our trip and look forward to catching up.

Warmest,
Milly

p.s. Have you guys seen that new code-breaking app for mobile devices? Fantastic!

TURN OVER ↘

Oh, there she goes again—enough about apps and mobile devices . . . Better, poetry!

> Though I get home how late, how late!
> So I get home, 'twill compensate.
> Better will be the ecstasy
> That they have done expecting me,
> When, night descending, dumb and dark,
> They hear my unexpected knock.

Looking forward to seeing you boys.

Yours,
Em

CRASH LANDING

PROFESSOR Perry drew nearer to the Poe twins, his attention fixed on the countdown clock as it moved from 5:20 to 5:19 to 5:18 to 5:17.

"Well?" the professor pressed the boys. "What's this countdown for?"

"Countdown?" Allan responded. "What countdown?"

Professor Perry gestured with the pistol. "The one right there on the screen!"

"Oh, that one," Edgar said, smiling. Then he gave the professor a look of false sympathy. "You may not like the answer."

"I'm growing impatient," the man said.

"It's a countdown to the crash landing of the Bradbury Telecommunications Satellite, which will occur right here at this mansion in"—Allan glanced back at the screen—"just about five minutes."

"What? How?" Professor Perry asked, furrowing his brow.

"We accessed the emergency guidance system and entered new coordinates, redirecting the satellite's trajectory," Edgar said.

"Here?" Professor Perry snapped. "Change it!"

Allan shook his head. "We can't. Gravity's taken over now."

"So I guess you could say that this is also a countdown to your—oh, what's the word?" Edgar searched his vocabulary. "Comeuppance."

"I'll tolerate no such thing!" the professor said, pointing the gun at him.

"Oh, I think you will," Edgar said confidently, as he could see what was going on behind the professor's back.

Uncle Jack had tiptoed into the room and picked up a piece of the broken sculpture, and now quietly moved toward the professor.

Professor Perry hesitated. Had he heard something? Was he just about to turn around?

Edgar wasn't taking any chances. "Professor Perry," he

said urgently. "Look what the countdown is doing now!"

The professor looked closer at the screen. It was merely counting down, just as before. "What?" he asked, confused.

This gave Uncle Jack just enough time to bring the big piece of sculpture down hard on the back of the professor's head, knocking the evil Edgar Allan Poe lookalike unconscious to the ground.

"Nice work, Uncle Jack," the boys said.

Uncle Jack beamed. "Oh, I'm still in my prime."

Aunt Judith and Roderick joined them.

The twins turned back to the computer screen: 4:42, 4:41 . . .

"What's the countdown?" asked Aunt Judith.

Uncle Jack had overheard the boys as he was creeping into the room. "It's how much time we have to get out of here before we're all toast."

"But we can't just walk downstairs and out the front door."

"So we climb out the window," Edgar told her.

"But we're on the second floor!" Aunt Judith objected.

"There's a ledge, so we'll find a way to shinny down," Allan assured her as he moved to the open window.

Roderick shot out onto the ledge. He loved this kind of stuff.

The twins moved next. "Follow us," they said to their aunt and uncle.

Aunt Judith took a deep breath. "I have a little fear of heights, but since you insist . . ." She hesitated. "You *are* insisting, right?"

"Right," Allan said, climbing out.

"We'll lead you down," Edgar reassured her, following his brother.

"OK." She climbed out onto the ledge. Uncle Jack brought up the rear.

Fortunately, ten feet along the ledge a lattice reached from the ground all the way to the roof.

"Just climb down like it's a ladder," Edgar called back to Aunt Judith.

"But lean in close to the building," Allan added, afraid that otherwise she might pull the lattice from the wall.

Once on the ground, the Poe family noticed a pinprick of light approaching from among the stationary stars in the eastern sky. In mere seconds, the pinprick grew proportionally to the size of a marble.

"Make a run for it," Uncle Jack said.

"We won't make it far enough on foot," Allan said.

"We need a car," Edgar elaborated.

"Let's go!" cried his brother.

The four Poes and Roderick raced to the front of the mansion, where the guests' cars were parked.

The only one that was unlocked was a vintage convertible roadster whose interior, even from a distance, smelled of perfume—Barbara Bainbridge's car.

Uncle Jack jumped into the driver's seat.

Aunt Judith slid into the passenger seat. Roderick settled on the floor at her feet.

Meantime, the boys pulled down the canvas top so that they could sit directly behind their guardians on the trunk, holding on to the metal luggage rack.

"No keys!" Uncle Jack shouted.

"No problem," Allan answered, racing around to the driver's side and reaching under the steering wheel column.

"Hot-wiring an older car is a snap," Edgar reassured his aunt and uncle.

Aunt Judith gave him a critical look. "When we get home, we're going to have a little talk about that, young man. Your uncle and I aren't raising any car thieves."

If we get home, Edgar thought, glancing into the sky, where the marble-size light had already grown, proportionally, to the size of a golf ball.

At that, the engine roared to life.

"What about everyone inside?" Allan asked.

"They all want to kill you!" Uncle Jack said, incredulous.

"We have to give them a fighting chance to get away, at least," Edgar said.

Uncle Jack answered by revving the engine, as if to say, *Hurry!*

The Poe twins turned and ran up the stairs to the mansion, through the big front door, and straight to the dining room. There, Professor Perry's nefarious guests, unaware of all the happenings, calmly enjoyed their reeking durian as they finished off the last of *many* bottles of eel wine.

The first to notice them was the professor's devoted henchman, Mr. Ian Archer, whom the boys had not seen since Kansas, when he was dressed as a flying monkey from *The Wizard of Oz*. "You two?" he shouted, his voice slurred.

Then Barbara Bainbridge stood up, likewise wobbly from too much wine. "Hey, I thought the drama was over."

Edgar and Allan shook their heads. "No, this is the climax," they said.

"Where's the professor?" a Chinese man asked.

"He's upstairs, unconscious," Allan answered. "You have to carry him down and get as far away from here as you can. *Now!*"

"Why?" demanded a shaven-headed man who was dressed like an undertaker.

"The satellite is going to crash into this mansion in less than two minutes," Edgar said.

The entire dinner party broke into laughter.

"And to think the professor described you brats as intelligent!" the actress said.

"The thing's hitting downtown Baltimore," the undertaker added. "We read about it on our phones."

"We changed the coordinates!" the boys cried, frustrated.

"It's some kind of trick," Mr. Ian Archer said, pulling a small pistol from a shoulder holster and pointing it first at one boy, then the other. "Let's see—*eeny . . . meeny . . . miney . . . moe!*" He fired.

Fortunately, he was too addled by eel wine to hit anything. But the boys didn't want to push their luck.

Besides, they hadn't any more time.

"You've been warned!" Allan shouted as the boys turned and ran.

What else could they do?

By the time they got outside, the descending satellite had grown proportionally from the size of a golf ball to that of a baseball. And it was getting bigger by the second!

"Hurry!" Aunt Judith called.

The twins jumped onto the back of the roadster, grabbing the luggage rack as Uncle Jack sped down the long gravel road.

The fiery baseball was now the size of a volleyball.

"Turn on your headlights, Jack!" cried Aunt Judith.

But by the time he found the switch, it wasn't necessary. Now the size of a beach ball, the satellite lit the night almost as brightly as day.

The temperature rose.

The snow all around began to melt.

"Go faster!" the boys yelled.

Uncle Jack shifted into high gear, tearing down the road.

The last things Edgar and Allan remembered were a blinding flash of light as the Bradbury Telecommunications Satellite crashed into the professor's mansion—and then the overpowering shock wave that hurled them from the speeding car, which skidded through the snow and smashed into the stone wall that surrounded the estate. The whole Poe family, including Roderick, were knocked unconscious even before the sound of the explosion reached them.

Was it some kind of concussion-induced dream?

Or did Edgar and Allan actually regain consciousness for a few fleeting moments where they lay, eight feet apart in a half-melted snowdrift?

Their parents stood over them, Mal and Irma Poe.

"We're so proud of you boys," their dad said, looking exactly as they remembered him.

"And we love you so much," their mom added, as pretty as ever.

The boys tried to sit up, but neither could move. Only their eyes and ears seemed to work.

"We've missed you every day, but you've never been out of our thoughts," Mom said.

And you've never been out of ours, the boys thought, though they couldn't speak.

"I'd so like to put my arms around you both." There were tears in her eyes.

"But you know how it works with ghosts," Dad added, also a little teary. "No touching."

But you're not going to have to be ghosts much longer, the twins thought.

Mom smiled, as if she had heard. "Yes, you've set us free," she said. "Thank you so much."

"And now you boys can be free too," added their father. "In your own lives."

Haven't we always been free?

"We love you, Edgar and Allan," their parents said, fading into the night.

WHAT THE POE TWINS DID NOT KNOW . . .
PHONE TEXT TO ALL GREEN SPRING VALLEY VOLUNTEER
FIREMEN AND EMERGENCY MEDICAL TECHS

CODE ZERO. Report to stations immediately. Massive impact and explosion at Willowtree Manor. First responders report car crash, with injuries, at the edge of estate grounds. Additional Baltimore County fire units currently responding. Repeat: CODE ZERO.

TWO NEW LIVES

THE city of Baltimore was saved.

But the professor's mansion was a mere crater in the snowy ground, still steaming three days later from the heat of the satellite's impact. The crash had registered a 4.5 on the Richter scale.

In the head trauma unit of Baltimore Memorial Hospital, Edgar and Allan simultaneously regained consciousness.

"What?" Edgar asked, startled and sitting up in his bed, unaware of where he was.

"How?" Allan murmured, equally confused.

Uncle Jack and Aunt Judith each sat at one boy's side in a wheelchair. Their heads were bandaged, and each had a pair of black eyes. He had splints on both wrists;

her ankle was in a cast. Still, they managed to smile at their nephews.

"Our boys are back!" Aunt Judith said, tears streaming down her cheeks.

"Poes are hearty folk," Uncle Jack said proudly.

The boys surveyed the small crowd that stood at the foot of their beds:

A beaming nurse in purple pants and a Hawaiian-print smock.

A white-haired, lab-coated doctor.

Stevie "The Hulk" Harrison, who held a bunch of flowers before him like a bride.

Mrs. Rosecrans, who, smiling, put her rosary beads into her purse.

And Em and Milly Dickinson, who looked pretty (each in her own way), but also a little tired, as if they'd been here a long time.

"Roderick is safe," Aunt Judith assured the twins.

"He'd be here, except that no cats are allowed in the hospital," said Uncle Jack.

"Sorry, boys," the doctor said at the twins' disappointed expressions.

Stevie came to their bedsides with his flowers. No one but the twins could see him unbutton the top of his shirt. Roderick's furry face popped out for just a moment to greet them, and then popped back inside, behind the flowers, before the medical staff could notice.

"You saved Baltimore," Aunt Judith said.

"The whole city is grateful," Uncle Jack added.

Suddenly, it all came back—the professor, the estate, the computer, the raven, the countdown, the escape out the window, the descending satellite, hot-wiring the roadster, the effort to save the professor's cohorts in the dining room, the careening drive away from the mansion, the satellite's impact, being thrown out of the convertible, hurtling through the air, blackness . . . and then, momentarily, their mom and dad.

"How long have we been unconscious?" Allan asked.

"Three days," the doctor answered.

"And in that time you solved a murder," Uncle Jack said.

Edgar and Allan looked at each other, confused.

"That note you brought out of the Perry mansion," their uncle continued, "was addressed to a scientist named M. Alexander Martin. Well, last week he was blown up in his office, and the note ties the crime to Professor Perry."

The boys had forgotten the note. And they'd never heard of M. Alexander Martin.

But solving a murder was never a bad thing.

"The bottom line is that you two saved Baltimore," Aunt Judith said.

"And what about Professor Perry and his . . . guests?" Allan asked, using the remote control device to bring his hospital bed to a more upright position.

Uncle Jack sighed. "They were all vaporized on impact."

"Oh," the boys said with mixed feelings.

"Hey, you'll never have to worry about any of them again."

"You warned them," Aunt Judith reassured her nephews.

"And you couldn't very well *carry* them out of the mansion," Uncle Jack added.

That was true.

The nurse approached. "How do you boys feel?"

"You mean physically?" Allan inquired.

The nurse nodded.

"Pretty good." Allan stretched his limbs.

Edgar wiggled his toes. "Me too."

"And other than physically?" the doctor asked.

"You mean psychologically?"

The doctor shrugged. "You could put it that way."

Allan considered this. "Hmmm, different from before," he said, a little surprised.

"Yeah," Edgar agreed.

"Different how?" Aunt Judith asked.

Edgar looked at Allan.

Allan looked at Edgar.

They didn't know how to answer because they'd

never felt this way before. Each strained for the words.

"I feel like . . . well, a computer whose hard drive has crashed and been reset," Allan said.

The doctor nodded sympathetically.

"That makes sense," murmured Milly Dickinson, who knew a lot about computers.

"And I feel like a leaf on an elm that has somehow passed through all the colors of the seasons and yet remains on the tree," Edgar said.

"That's beautifully put," volunteered Em, the more poetically inclined of the Dickinson sisters.

"So you feel like a broken computer?" the doctor asked Allan, narrowing his eyes analytically.

"No, no. That's not what I meant."

Milly pushed past the doctor and toward Allan's bed. "I think I understand," she said, fixing Allan with her brown eyes. "Now that you feel reset, you also feel disoriented, as if your operating system was updated while your hard drive was down."

"Exactly!" he said, noticing happily that Milly had rested her hand on the hospital bed not too far from his own.

The doctor didn't seem to follow. "And you feel like a leaf?" he asked Edgar.

Edgar shook his head emphatically. "It's not that simple."

Em moved toward Edgar. "Could it be that even though your leaf on the tree has passed through all the seasons it remains the same, while it is the elm that has regenerated and become new?"

"Yes!" Edgar answered, admiring Em's quick understanding of poetic metaphor.

Confused, the doctor turned to the boys' friends and family. "Are they describing the same feeling?" he asked.

"Almost," Edgar said, before anyone else could speak.

"But not quite," Allan added.

"How's it different?" asked Aunt Judith.

"Well, Edgar feels his way and I feel mine," Allan answered simply.

"That's to be expected," the doctor affirmed.

But wait . . .

The boys looked at each other again. How could they be feeling *different*?

They were two boys with one mind, weren't they?

Yet Edgar realized that, since waking, he hadn't known what Allan was thinking, feeling, or seeing.

And Allan was as much in the dark about Edgar.

"What's your favorite kind of ice cream?" Edgar asked

his brother, elevating his bed so that when they turned their heads they were eye to eye.

Allan answered automatically. "Rocky road, of course."

It had always been their favorite.

"Wait, no," he amended slowly. "Actually, I think my favorite is pistachio. Yours?"

"Mint chocolate chip," Edgar said without hesitation.

"Do you boys want ice cream?" the nurse cut in. "We can do that."

The twins ignored her.

"Are we . . . two separate boys now?" Allan asked his brother.

"I think maybe we are," Edgar answered.

"What do you mean by that?" the doctor asked.

The Poe twins didn't have to be psychically linked to know they'd never make the doctor understand.

"Never mind," Allan said.

The twins had never understood why they'd been like two boys with one mind. They'd just always known each other's thoughts, been able to unravel problems many times faster than other human beings. Professor Perry had called it "quantum entanglement," and, though he had been evil and deranged, Perry wasn't stupid.

And here was another problem Edgar and Allan couldn't unravel: why had their mysterious connection ended?

Was it the massive impact of the crashing satellite?

Was it their three days spent unconscious?

Was it exposure to some kind of outer space contamination from the explosion?

Did it have something to do with their parents' ghosts?

Could this be what their dad had meant about their being free?

Each boy's mind remained razor-sharp, even if they might both be a nanosecond slower when dividing numbers like 278 by 277 to the ninth digit or picking up dead languages like ancient Greek.

Together, they had been a remarkable force. But might being separate boys bring opportunities?

For example, being brothers in a whole new way.

"Hi, Edgar," said Allan, as if for the first time.

"Hi, Allan."

"By the way, pistachio ice cream is only good for nuts," Edgar said good-naturedly.

Allan grinned. "Mint chocolate chip isn't even good enough to feed livestock!"

Both boys laughed.

Though neither knew it, Edgar and Allan Poe shared their last perfectly simultaneous thought at that very moment.

I am my own boy. Wow, what possibilities!

Mr. Poe in the Great Beyond

Mr. Poe had been summoned to Mr. Shakespeare's office on the 184,692,384th floor of the celestial office building. Generally, such a summons led to a demotion.

Mr. Poe didn't know what was lower than the Animal Languages Division, but as he approached the office, he didn't care. He was overjoyed by the events of the last few days. His beloved nephews safe at last, and their parents freed from their orbiting tomb! In this light, nothing that his superiors might do to punish him could alter his sense of accomplishment and his newly found peace of mind.

So he knocked on the door of Mr. Shakespeare's office with a jaunty rhythm.

"Enter," Mr. Shakespeare called.

Mr. Poe walked in to find something altogether unexpected.

Standing beside Mr. Shakespeare's large desk was Homer, the Greek father of Western literature, who ran the entire Arts Division. On the far side of the wide room, near the tall, wall-length bookshelf (filled exclusively with translations of Mr. Shakespeare's plays) were Mr. Walt Whitman and Miss Emily Dickinson, Mr. Poe's best work friends. Near the window, admiring the view—quite impressive from almost two hundred million floors up—were the kindly, nineteenth-century couple Genevieve and Clarence Du Valier, whom the Poe twins had set free from two centuries of haunting the Saint Louis Cemetery in New Orleans. And, rising from the couch, where they'd been sitting hand in hand, were Mal and Irma Poe, the building's newest and most grateful inhabitants. Mr. Shakespeare rose from his desk chair.

They all turned to Mr. Poe.

Everyone held a glass of champagne.

"Come in, Mr. Poe," Mr. Shakespeare said. "Please."

Mr. Poe closed the door behind him and took a few steps forward.

"I know I've been rather hard on you of late," Mr. Shakespeare said. "But sometimes adversity brings out the best in a man or woman. And your latest bending of our rules—I'm referring, of course, to your talking raven—well, it *was* brilliant."

This from Mr. Shakespeare, of all people!

Mal and Irma stepped toward Mr. Poe.

Mal, who bore a strong family resemblance, held out his hand. The two men shook. "We couldn't ask for a better ancestor than you," he said humbly.

Next, Irma threw her arms around Mr. Poe.

At first, he was taken aback by the warmth of the contact, but after a moment he allowed it to sink in.

It felt good.

"Mr. Poe here is our number one rule-breaker," Homer said to the gathered friends and colleagues. "But," he added, "there are times when doing the right thing is more important than doing the officially approved thing. Not often, mind you. But in rare instances of the utmost importance."

Mr. Shakespeare handed Mr. Poe a glass of champagne.

"And so," Homer continued, "in that spirit, allow me to offer a toast to Mr. Edgar Allan Poe."

Everyone raised their glasses.

"To Mr. Poe!" they said before drinking.

Mr. Poe looked at Mr. Shakespeare. "So I'm not demoted?"

Mr. Shakespeare laughed. "On the contrary, you've been promoted upstairs."

"To the penthouse," Homer explained. "On the grounds of extreme courage, selflessness, and ingenuity."

Mr. Poe could hardly believe the good news.

He had never imagined that his time here on the working floors of the celestial skyscraper, the "middle place," might come to such a fortuitous end. And so suddenly!

Mr. Shakespeare strode across the room. "Please accept my deepest respect, Mr. Poe."

They shook hands.

"And allow me to apologize for sometimes being such a surly, onion-eyed malt-worm," the bard continued.

"Oh, you do yourself an injustice, Mr. Shakespeare," Mr. Poe responded with a sly grin. "I never found you to be 'onion-eyed.'"

Mr. Shakespeare took the rebuke with good humor.

"Of course, in the penthouse you'll have no more professional responsibilities," Homer explained. "You'll exist in a continual state of peace and bliss."

Mr. Poe shrugged, embarrassed by his good fortune.

But something nagged at him.

"What if . . . what if I don't actually want to leave here?" he asked slowly.

Homer couldn't hide the surprise on his bearded face. "Why in Zeus's name not?"

Mr. Poe wasn't sure that a continual state of peace and bliss would be quite to his liking. For one thing, it would never give him anything to write about. And there was another thing . . . He glanced in the direction of Miss Emily Dickinson.

Everyone noticed—including Emily herself, who blushed crimson.

"I suppose your staying could be arranged," Mr. Shakespeare said helpfully.

"I could go back to writing fortune cookies," Mr. Poe offered.

Homer laughed. "Oh, that wouldn't be necessary."

"If you stay, you can have a corner office on this floor, Mr. Poe," Mr. Shakespeare said, slapping him on the back. "Just like mine. Fantastic view. And you can write whatever you want."

"Whatever I want?" He could practice his true calling!

Homer nodded.

"Why do you think Homer and I are still here?" Mr. Shakespeare asked rhetorically.

"I didn't even know you two were still at it," Mr. Poe said.

"I just completed a new epic poem," Homer acknowledged. "It's better than *The Iliad* and *The Odyssey* put together!"

"And I've been writing plays," Mr. Shakespeare chimed in. "Tragedy, comedy, history, pastoral,

pastoral-comical, historical-pastoral, tragical-historical, tragical-comical-historical-pastoral, scene individable, poem unlimited—"

"I'll stay," Mr. Poe interrupted, wary that Mr. Shakespeare might go on forever.

"Good," his former boss said sincerely.

"And what do you think your first new work will be about?" Homer asked Mr. Poe.

He didn't need even a moment to consider.

"Twin boys, whose story will make for quite a book," he said.

THE END

ACKNOWLEDGMENTS

My heartfelt thanks to those who journeyed from beginning to end with Edgar, Allan, and me. First, to my agent, Kelly Sonnack, who saw the possibilities of an early draft and steadfastly helped me to realize and exceed those possibilities; to Sharyn November, editor extraordinaire, whose creative spirit is as vast as the night sky through which the Bradbury Telecommunications Satellite so recently orbited; to Sam Zuppardi, whose drawings jump off the page with energy, warmth, and humor; to Eileen Savage, designer, who made the books look more beautiful than I imagined possible; to Tara Shanahan for spreading the word that Edgar and Allan were out there in the world; to director Tony Hudz and actor Arte Johnson, who together made the audio versions of the Misadventures of Edgar and Allan Poe trilogy dramatic, funny, and unique. I know how fortunate I am to have worked with such wonderful people. My gratitude and best wishes to all of you.

I am grateful also to Robert Arthur Jr. (1909–1969), a veteran writer of the golden age of radio, who introduced a book series for young readers in the 1960s, "Alfred Hitchcock and the Three Investigators," which captivated my nine-year-old imagination and inspired me to start writing stories myself. And to the great Robert Louis Stevenson, who demonstrated that an author can write well for more than one audience, more than one age group—that good writing is, simply, good writing. And to the Beatles, just because.

Finally, to Julie, my love and gratitude for your living so graciously with the ups and downs of my sometimes chaotic writing life.

—G. M.

Thanks again to Gordon, the mastermind behind this whole fabulous misadventure, and to Kelly and Sharyn, who added their own magic to the crazy scheme and let me be an accomplice. To Nancy and Eileen for making it all look so pretty; to Tom and Lucy, who have been good friends to the Poe Boys over the past three years and even better friends to me for a lot longer than that; to Rob Baines for clearing out his attic and giving me the fountain pen he found there—I used it to draw these pictures! And thanks again to my family—mum and dad, Nic, Luisa, grandparents, and everyone who followed things from the beginning. And of course thanks to beautiful Jade—my fiancée!—for pretty much everything else.

—S. Z.